_L_ove's Long
Journey

Love's Long Journey

JANETTE OKE

LOVE'S LONG JOURNEY
A Bethany House Publication/June 1982
The Janette Oke Collection/1997

Cover by Dan Thornberg, Bethany House staff artist.

Bethany House Publishers
A Ministry of Bethany Fellowship, Inc.
11300 Hampshire Avenue South
Minneapolis, Minnesota 55438

If you would be interested in purchasing additional copies of this book,
please write to this address for information:

The Janette Oke Collection
BDD Direct, Inc.
1540 Broadway
New York, NY 10036

ISBN: 0-553-80565-7

BDD Direct, Inc., 1540 Broadway, New York, New York 10036

Printed in the United States of America

1 3 5 7 9 10 8 6 4 2

This book is dedicated to you, the
readers of *Love Comes Softly* and
Love's Enduring Promise, with
thanks for your kind words of
encouragement.

Table of Contents

Prologue

Imagine if you can the grief of family separation back in the days of the pioneers.

For weeks and months the entire family would have been in a fever-pitch of excitement and activity. Plans were made, clothing and bedding were sewn, crates and crocks were packed and supplies were purchased or prepared, sufficient for many months, or even years. Consider packing all that food, from coffee to flour, from lard to honey, from molasses to salt—pickled, salted, dried, canned. There were lamps and the fuel needed for them, grease for the wagons, repair parts for the harnesses, besides guns and gunpowder, tools, nails, rope, crocks, kettles, pots and pans, dishes, medicines, seeds, clothing, and material to make more when those wore out. Any furniture or equipment that the family could afford and find room for was packed in the wagons; a stove, sewing machine, bed, chairs, table—they all had to be taken along.

The packing was done carefully. Breakables were packed in sawdust and crated in handmade boxes. Many items needed to be protected against possible water damage, for there were rivers to be forded and rains to be endured. The crates would be unpacked at journey's end and disassembled; every board would be carefully hoarded for some future building project—a window frame, a stool, a small crib. The sawdust would be used sparingly to feed a fire, sprinkled lightly over the smoking buffalo chips.

The crocks and jars containing foods they had carried west would be re-used after they had yielded up their store.

Yes, it was a monumental task. The preparation for such a move must have taxed bodies and emotions to the limit.

But when the sorting and packing was finished, the wagons were loaded and the teams were hitched and ready to move out—what then?

Mothers and fathers bade their offspring farewell with the knowledge that they might be seeing them for the last time. There was almost no means of communication, should the need arise; from then on they would know next to nothing of their whereabouts or their well-being. Many families who stayed behind hoped that they would never hear—for only bad news was of sufficient import to be carried across the empty miles.

Wife followed husband, convinced that her rightful place was by his side regardless of the strong tug that pulled her to the home that she had known and loved. Danger, loneliness, and possible disaster awaited them in the new world that they were entering, but she went regardless.

I have often thought about those pioneer women. What it must have cost many of them to follow their men! To venture forth, leaving behind the things that represented security and safety; to birth their babies unattended; to nurse sick children with no medicines or doctors; to be mother, teacher, minister, physician, tailor and supermarket to a growing family; to support, without complaint, their men through floods, blizzards, sandstorms and droughts; to walk tall when there was little to wear, little to work with and even less to eat.

God bless them all—the women who courageously went forth with their men. And those who stood with tear-filled eyes and aching hearts and let them go. God bless their memory. And grant to us a measure of the strength, courage, love and determination that prompted them to do what they did.

Janette Oke

Chapter 1

The Journey Begins

Missie experimentally pushed back her bonnet and let the rays of the afternoon sun fall directly on her already too-warm head. She wasn't sure which was preferable—the loss of protection from the sun that the bonnet had provided or the shade from the wide brim that also kept the slight breeze from her face. It was hot! She comforted herself by reasoning that the worst of the day's heat was already past; surely it would begin to cool before long as the sun's rays waned.

Her first day on the trail had seemed extremely long. To Missie the excitement of the morning seemed already weeks past. But no, time insisted that it truly had been only at the dawning of this very day.

As she recalled the early events of the morning, Missie again felt a tingle go through her. She and Willie were really heading west! After all of the planning and dreaming, they were actually on the way. It still seemed a dream, yet Missie's weary, aching body verified that it was fact.

She shifted on the hard, wooden boards of the bumping wagon

to gain what she hoped would be a more comfortable position. Willie turned to her, his hands on the reins still aware of every movement of the plodding team.

"Ya tirin'?" he asked, his eyes on her flushed face.

Missie smiled and pushed back some strands of damp hair. "A bit. 'Bout time for me to stretch my legs again, I reckon."

Willie nodded and turned back to the horses he was driving.

"I miss ya when yer gone, but I sure won't deny ya none any relief that ya might be getting from a walk now an' then. Ya wantin' down now?"

"In a few minutes." Missie fell silent.

Willie stole an anxious sideways glance at her. She looked content enough.

"Sure's one bustlin', dusty way to travel, this wagon train-in,'" Missie commented. "Harness creakin', horses stompin', people shoutin'! Hadn't realized thet it would be so noisy-like."

"I 'spect that it'll quieten some as we all get used to it."

"Yeah, I reckon so."

Missie reached out to tuck a small hand under Willie's arm. She could feel his muscles tighten and ripple as they gave firm guidance to the team. His coarse cotton shirt was damp in many places and Missie noticed that he had undone a couple of buttons at the neck.

"Guess we sorta just brought our noise and bustle along with us," she said.

"Meanin'?"

"Well, you know what it's been like at home for all these weeks that we've been a plannin', packin', cratin', loadin'— seemed it would never end. An' the noise was really somethin'— everybody talkin' at once, hammers poundin', an' barrels an' pans bangin'. It was a madhouse, that's what it was."

Willie laughed. "Was kinda, wasn't it?"

Silence again.

Willie again stole a glance at Missie and this time he could see a shadow cloud her bright blue eyes. He waited for a few moments. When Missie made no further comment, Willie spoke cautiously.

"Ya seem to be thinkin' awful deep-like."

Missie allowed a quiet sigh to escape from her and tightened her grip on Willie's arm. "Not deep—just thinkin' of home. It must seem awfully quiet there now. Awfully quiet. After all the days an' months of gettin' ready—" lost in thought, Missie didn't finish her sentence. Watching her preoccupation, Willie did not interrupt her reverie.

Missie thought of their two wagons crammed full. Never had she dreamed it possible to get so much into two wagons. Everything that they would be needing in the months ahead had been loaded into those wagons—and a fair number of things that they could very well have lived without if they had had to, Missie realized. She thought especially of the fancy dishes that her ma had purchased with some of her own egg money and insisted on packing in sawdust herself. "Someday you'll be glad thet ya made the room," Marty assured her; and Missie knew in her heart that someday she would indeed look at the dishes and ache with the sad joy that they brought to her soul.

A sense of sadness had overtaken Missie and she had no desire to have Willie read her mind. The thoughts of home and loved ones brought a sharp pain somewhere deep inside of her. If she wasn't careful she'd be in tears. She swallowed hard and forced a smile.

"Maybe I should get me in a little more walkin' now," she said briskly.

"I'll pull over right up there ahead at thet widenin' in the road," he promised.

Missie nodded.

"Have you noticed that we are already beyond the farms that we know?" Willie asked.

"I've noticed."

"Makes it seem more real-like. Like we really are a-goin' West." She shared the joy and excitement in Willie's voice, but at the same instance that now-familiar pain twisted within her. She was going West with Willie—but she was leaving behind all others that she loved. When would she see them again? *Would* she see them again—ever? The tears pressed against the back of her eyes.

She was glad when Willie pulled the team over for a brief stop so that she could climb down over the wagon wheel. The dust whirled up as Willie moved on again, and Missie stepped away a few paces and turned her back; she pulled her bonnet back up into position to keep the dust from settling on her hair. She waited until the wagons had passed her, then looked around for someone that she might have already met among the walkers that followed the teams. There didn't seem to be anyone that she recognized at hand, so Missie smiled at those closest to her and, without a word, took position in the group.

As she walked the dusty, rutted road, her body, though young and healthy, hurt all over. She wondered how the older ladies were able to keep going. She glanced about her at two women walking slightly to her right. *They look 'bout Mama's age*, she mused. *Mama is well and strong an' can most times outwork me; still, I wouldn't want to see her have to put in such a day.*

The women did look tired, and Missie's heart went out to them. Suddenly, relieved, Missie now remembered the words of the wagon master, Mr. Blake, when he had given them their orders that morning. At the time it had seemed foolishness to Missie to even consider a short day the first few days on the trail. Now she began to understand the wisdom in Mr. Blake's pronouncement. How glad she would be to stop.

Missie's thoughts returned to Willie. She wondered if he would welcome the early camp tonight or if his eagerness to reach their destination would make him want to push on.

Missie was proud of Willie, proud of his manly good looks— his dark head of slightly curling hair, his deep brown eyes, his strong chin with its indentation akin to a dimple (though Willie would never allow her to call it such), his well-shaped nose that had been narrowly spared perfection by his fall from a tree when he was nine years old—these things were her Willie. So were the broad shoulders, the tall frame, the strong arms.

But when Missie thought of Willie, she pictured not only the man that others saw but his character that she had come to know so well. Willie who seemed to read her thoughts, who considered others first, who was flexible when dealing with others but steadfast when dealing with himself; this man who was strong and purposeful in his decisions—a mite stubborn, some felt, but

Missie preferred to describe him as "firm." Well, maybe a *little* stubborn, she conceded, if being stubborn was hanging onto a dream—his dream of raising cattle, of working with fine horses, of owning his own ranch, of going further west.

When Willie had made his trip west, alone, to find his spread two years previously, he had persevered through seemingly endless searching and red tape until he actually held in his hand the title deed for the land. When their going had been delayed in order to set aside the money needed for the venture, Willie had chafed, but his dream had not died. He had worked hard at the mill, laying aside every penny that they could spare until he felt sure that they had saved enough. Missie had been proud to add whatever she could from her teacher's salary to make the sum grow more quickly. It gave her a sense of having a part in Willie's dream. It was now becoming her dream, too.

Missie's glance lifted to the sky to figure out the time by the sun. It was somewhere between three and four o'clock, she reasoned.

At home, the time of day was easily distinguished by the activity that was evident. Right now her ma would be taking a break from heavier tasks by spending some time in her favorite chair with mending or knitting. Her pa would still be in the field. They, too, had been so generous in adding to Willie's little nest egg. She thought of the final moments with her parents.

They had been so brave as they had bid her good-byes that morning. Clark had gathered them all close around him and led them in family prayer. Marty had tried desperately not to cry. At Missie's, "It's all right Mama—go ahead and cry, iffen you want to," the tears came; the two held one another close and cried, and they felt some measure of relief and comfort come to their hearts.

Missie now brushed away unbidden tears and glanced about to see if she had been observed. Deliberately she pushed the thoughts of loneliness from her. If she wasn't careful she'd work herself into a real state and go into camp with red-rimmed eyes and blotchy cheeks. Besides, she had Willie; she need never be *truly* lonesome.

Missie trudged on, placing one tired foot before the other. Even in her sturdy walking shoes, her feet looked small and the plain brown cotton frock did not hide the youthfulness of her lithe body. She raised a hand to push away blonde hair that had come untucked and insisted upon wisping about her face. Strands of it clung to the dampness of her moist forehead. Her normally fair cheeks were flushed from the heat of the day. In spite of her homesickness, weariness, and the hot sun overhead, her clear, bright eyes sparkled with enthusiasm and excitement as they swept back and forth in a effort to miss nothing.

Missie's attention was drawn back to her traveling companions. Some of the women were now gathering dry sticks and twigs as they followed the wagons. They had a number of their children running here and there, picking up suitable fuel as well. *They must be anticipating stopping soon*, Missie thought; she too began to look about as she walked, gathering fuel for her own fire.

A commotion ahead brought Missie's attention back to the wagons. The drivers were breaking line and maneuvering into a circle as they had been instructed that morning. Missie's step became lighter. It wouldn't be long now until she would be resting in some shade. How glorious it would be just to sit down for a spell and let the afternoon breeze cool her warm head and body! She was anxious, also, to chat with Willie and see how he had fared in the short time that they had been apart.

Missie wondered, with a fluttering of her pulse, if tonight, by their campfire would be the time to tell Willie about her growing convictions that *perhaps* they were to become parents. She was quite sure now, though she still had not mentioned it to Willie. *Don't want to raise false hopes*, she had told herself.

Would Willie be pleased? She knew how he loved younguns, and she knew his eagerness to have a son of his own; but she could also guess his concern for her. He had hoped to make the trip West and be settled in their own home *before* a family arrived. A long wagon trip could be very difficult for an expectant mother. Yes, Willie *might* feel that the coming baby had picked an inappropriate time to be making an appearance.

Missie had no such misgivings. She was young and healthy and, besides, they would reach Willie's land long before the baby was due. Still, she had to admit to herself that she had put off telling Willie her suspicions until they were actually on the trail.

She had been somewhat afraid that if he knew, he would have suggested postponing their journey and to Missie's thinking, he had suffered enough delay already.

So she kept her precious secret. She hadn't dared even whisper it to her mother, though her whole being ached to do so. *She'd fret*, Missie told herself. *She'd never rest easy for one night while we were on the trail.*

Missie spotted their wagons side-by-side in the big circle. Willie was unhitching the team from their first wagon, and Henry Klein, their hired driver, was working with the second team. It had become evident weeks before, when they had begun to load, that one wagon was not going to be sufficient for living quarters on the way, plus a transport for all their needed supplies. Missie's father, Clark, had suggested the second wagon, and had even helped in locating a driver. Other members of the wagon train also had more than one wagon moving West. Most of them were fortunate enough to have another family member who could drive the teams.

As Missie neared the train, she surveyed the closing circle. The last wagon, the twenty-seventh, moved into position to complete it.

Missie approached Willie now and responded to his grin with a smile of her own.

"Been a long day—yer lookin' tired," he said with concern.

"I am a bit—the sun's been so hot, and fer sure it takes the starch outa one."

"It's time fer a good rest. Bit of that shade should revive ya some. Ya wantin' me to bring ya a stool or a blanket from the wagon?"

"I'll do it. You have the team to care for."

"Mr. Blake says there's a stream jest beyond that stand of timber there. We're gonna take all the stock down fer a drink an' then tether them in the draw. Blake says there's grass a-plenty there."

"What time you be wantin' supper?" Missie asked.

"Not fer a couple hours anyway. Ya got plenty of time fer a rest."

"I'll need me more firewood. I didn't start gatherin' soon

enough. That little bit that I brought in won't last no time."

"No rush fer a fire either. I'll bring some wood back with me. Henry won't mind bringing some, too. Ya jest git a little time outa thet hot sun fer awhile—ya look awfully tuckered out." Willie's voice was anxious.

"It's just the excitement and strangeness of it all, I expect. I'll get used to it. But right now I think I'll take a bit of rest in the shade of those trees. I'll be as good as new when I can get off my feet some."

Willie left with the horses and the two milk cows that had been tied behind the wagons; Missie went for a blanket to throw down on the ground in the shade of the trees.

She felt guilty as she lowered herself onto the blanket. All of the other women already seemed to be busy with something. Well, she'd just rest a short while and then she would busy herself as well. For the moment it felt good just to sit.

Missie leaned back comfortably against the trunk of a tree and closed her eyes, turning her head slightly so that she could take full advantage of the gentle breeze. It teased at the loose strands of her hair and fanned her flushed face. How she ached! All of her bones seemed to cry out for a warm, relaxing soak in a tub. If she were home . . . but Missie quickly put that thought away from her. Her folks' big white house with its homey kitchen and wide stairway was no longer *her* home. The upstairs room with its cheerful rugs and frilly curtains was no longer *her* room. She was totally Willie's responsibility now, and Willie was hers. She prayed a short prayer that she would be worthy of such a man as her Willie—that God would help her to make a home for him that was filled with happiness and love. And then her eyes still closed, she felt the achiness weighing her whole body down on the blanket.

Ignore it, she commanded herself. *Ignore it, and it will go away.*

Chapter 2

Day's End

When Missie opened her eyes again she was surprised at the changes that had taken place around her. It was much cooler now and the sun that had shone down with such intense heat during the day was now hanging, friendly and placid, low in the western sky.

The smell of woodsmoke was heavy in the air—a sharp, pleasant smell; and the odors of cooking food and boiling coffee made her insides twinge with hunger. Now fully awake, she looked around in embarrassment at the supper preparations. Surely every woman in the whole train had been busy and about while she slept. What must they think of her? Willie would soon be back from caring for the animals—and not even find a fire started!

Missie hurried toward her wagons, swishing out her skirts and smoothing back her hair.

It took a moment for her to realize that the fire that burned directly in front of their wagons was *her* fire, and that the delicious smell of stew and coffee came from *her* own cooking pots.

She was trying to sort it all out when Willie poked his head out the wagon. His face still showed concern when he looked at her, but changed quickly to a look of relief. "Yer lookin' better. How ya feelin'?"

Missie stammered some, "I'm fine—truly, just fine." Then she added in a lowered voice, "But shamed nigh to death."

"Shamed?" Willie's voice sounded unnecessarily loud to Missie. " 'Bout what?"

"Well—me sittin' there a-sleepin' in the middle of the day, an' you—you makin' the fire, an' the coffee an'—my goodness—what must they all think of me—that my husband has to do his work an' mine too?"

"Iffen thet's all thet's troublin' ya," Willie responded, "I reckon we can learn to live with it. 'Sides, I didn't make the fire. Henry did. He was mighty anxious fer his supper. Boy, can thet fella eat! We're liable to have to butcher both of those cows jest to feed 'im, long before we reach where we're goin'."

"Henry's eaten?"

"Sure has. I think he even left us a little bit. Seemed in a big hurry to be off. There jest happens to be a couple of young girls travelin' with this train. Think maybe Henry went to sorta get acquainted-like." Willie winked.

"Aren't ya comin' out?" Missie asked when Willie made no move to leave the wagon.

"I'm lookin' fer the bread. Can't find a thing in all these crocks, cans an' boxes. Where'd ya put it, anyway? Henry wolfed down his food without it, but I'd sorta like a bit of bread to go with my supper."

Missie laughed. "Really!" she said, shaking her head, "bet ya near took a bite of it. It's right there, practically under your nose." She clambered into the wagon. "Here, let me get it. Mama sent some of her special tarts for our first night out, too."

As Missie lifted the bread and the butter tarts from the crock in which they had been stored, another tug pulled at her somewhere deep inside. She could envision Marty's flushed face as she bent over her oven, removing the special baking for the young couple that she loved so dearly.

Willie seemed to sense Missie's mood; his arms went round

her and he pulled her close.

"She'll be missin' you too, long 'bout now," he said softly against her hair.

Missie swallowed hard. "I reckon she will," she whispered.

"Missie?" Willie hesitated. "Are ya sure? It's still not too late to turn back, ya know. Iffen yer in doubt. . . ?" Iffen ya feel—?"

"My goodness, no," Missie said emphatically. "There's not a doubt in my mind at all. I'm lookin' forward to seein' yer land and buildin' a home. You know that! Sure, I'll miss Mama an' Pa an' the family—'specially at first. But I just gotta grow up, that's all. Everyone's gotta grow up *sometime*." How could Willie think that she was so selfish as to deny him his dream?

"Yer sure?"

"I'm sure."

"It won't be an easy trip—you know thet."

"I know."

"An' it won't be easy even after we git there. There's no house yet, no neighbors, no church. You'll miss it all, Missie."

"I'll have you."

Willie pulled her back into his arms. "I'm afraid I'm not much to make up fer all thet you're losin'. But I love ya, Missie—I love ya so much."

"Then that's all I need," whispered Missie. "Love is the one thing thet I reckon I jest couldn't do without, so—" she reached up and kissed him on his chin. "As long as you love me, I should make out just fine."

Missie drew back gently from Willie's arms. "We'd better be eatin' that supper you cooked. I'm powerful hungry."

Willie nodded. "But you might change yer mind once you've tasted my cookin'." They both laughed.

After they had finished their meal together and Missie had washed up the few dishes, Willie brought out their Bible. It was carefully wrapped in oiled paper with an inner wrap of soft doeskin.

"Been thinkin'," he said. "Our mornin's are goin' to be short and rushed; it might be easier fer us to have our readin' time at night."

Missie nodded and settled down beside him. It was still light enough to see, but the light would not last for long. Willie found his place and began in an even voice.

"Fear thou not; for I am with thee: be not dismayed; for I am thy God: I will strengthen thee; yea, I will help thee; yea, I will uphold thee with the right hand of my righteousness."*

He closed the Bible slowly.

"Yer pa underlined thet for us. When he handed me the Bible this morning, he read it to me and marked it with this red ribbon. He said fer us to claim thet verse fer our own and to read it every day, if need be, until we felt it real and meaningful in our hearts."

"It's a good verse," Missie said. Her voice was tremulous. If she closed her eyes she was sure that she would be able to see her pa sitting at the kitchen table with the family Bible opened before him and all of the family gathered round. She could even hear his voice as he led them in the morning prayer time. Her pa—the spiritual leader of the home. No . . . not anymore. Willie was the head of her home now; he was her spiritual leader. Now she would look to him for strength and direction to get her through each day—whether happy or difficult. She was not Clark's little girl anymore; she was a woman, a woman and a wife. Clark had handed her into the care and keeping of Willie; and though Missie was sure that her father's love and prayers would reach out to her always, she also knew that Clark was content in his knowledge that she had taken her rightful place in life . . . by Willie's side.

Missie reached for Willie's hand and clung to it as they prayed together. Willie thanked God for being with them through the day and for the love of those left behind. He prayed for comfort for their hearts at this difficult time, as he and Missie learned to live without the nearness of their families; he asked for safety as they traveled and for special strength for Missie in the long days ahead, his voice tight again with concern. Missie determined that tonight was not the time to share her secret. There was no need to trouble Willie. She'd wait until she had gotten used to the bumping and the walking and had toughened to the

*Isaiah 41:10, KJV.

pace of the trail. Besides, she told herself, there was still a chance that she could be wrong.

If she was right—and deep down inside, Missie admitted the fact that indeed she must be—she was bound to gain new vigor and strength with each passing day. In fact, the fresh air and exercise was bound to be good for her. She'd wait. She'd wait until Willie could see for himself that she was healthy and strong, and then she'd tell her secret. Then he would be as excited over the coming event as she was.

Oh, if only she could have told her ma and pa. She would have looked into their faces and exclaimed with joy, "I think you're gonna be Grandma an' Grandpa—now, what do ya think of that?" They would have hugged and laughed and cried together in one grand tangle of happiness. It would have been so much fun to announce her good news. But that wasn't to be—and it wasn't the right time to announce it to Willie either. She'd wait.

Chapter 3

Another Day

Missie stirred herself with difficulty, unconsciously testing her back, her legs, her arms, to see just how much pain the movement brought to her. How she ached! Her mind reached for the reason. As sleep left her, it all came back to her with a fresh wave, a mixture of excitement and misgivings. They were on the trail. They were headed west and she had been jostled until she could stand it no more and then had walked behind the wagons until her body protested with every step; and now, after a sleep on the hard, confined bed in their new living quarters, she ached even more.

Willie must hurt too, she thought. She reached for him but her hand touched only his deserted pillow. Willie had already quietly left the cramped, canvas-covered wagon that was to be their home for many weeks.

Missie quickly pulled herself from her bed, suppressing a groan as she did so. "S'pose I've gone an' done it again," she muttered. "Willie likely had to cook his own breakfast too."

But after Missie quickly dressed and climbed stiffly down from the wagon, she was relieved to find that the sun was just

24

casting its first rays of golden light over the eastern horizon—very few people were stirring about the camp. Willie had started a fire and left it burning for her. Missie added a couple of sticks and watched as the flames accepted them with crackling eagerness.

"Land sakes!" Missie exclaimed. "I wonder iffen I'll ever get my tied-up muscles all unwound." She began to pace back and forth, flinging and flexing her arms to limber them up. "Me, a farm girl, and so pampered that one good day's walkin' bothers me! Guess Mama didn't work me hard enough."

As Missie stamped back and forth, she recognized another good reason for keeping on the move. In the coolness of the morning, the mosquitoes were out in droves and they all seemed to be hungry. Missie decided to return to the wagon for a long-sleeved sweater to protect her arms.

She poured a generous amount of river water from the two-gallon bucket into the washbasin that sat on the shelf on the outside of the wagon; she then began her morning wash. The water was cold and Missie was relieved to reach for the rough towel to rub the warmth back into her face and hands. But she did feel refreshed and ready to begin her day. She draped the towel over its peg and busied herself with the breakfast preparations. The coffee was bubbling and the bacon and eggs sending forth their early-morning "all's well" signal when Henry made his appearance.

Missie thought of Henry as no more than a boy, but smiled to herself as she realized that he was at least as old as her Willie. *Still*, she thought, *he doesn't have the same grown-up manner that Willie possesses.*

"Mornin', Henry."

"Mornin', Ma'am."

The "Ma'am" brought another smile to Missie's lips.

"Hungry?"

Henry grinned. "Sure am."

"Did you sleep well?"

"Pesky mosquitoes don't let nothin' sleep. Bet the horses had to swish and stomp all night."

"Didn't bother me none. Leastways not until I got up this

morning. Maybe we didn't have any in our wagon."

"Willie said thet they were botherin' him."

Missie looked up from turning the bacon. "That so? Me, I never even paid them no mind. Guess I was just sleepin' too sound to notice. Where is Willie?"

"We checked out the horses and the cows, an' then he went over to have a chat with Mr. Blake."

"Everything all right?" She looked up with a furrowed brow.

"Right as rain. Willie jest wanted to chat a spell, I reckon—to see how far we be goin' today."

"Oh." There was relief in Missie's voice. She didn't have to worry. She began to set out the tin plates for the morning meal.

It wasn't long until she heard the sound of Willie's familiar whistling. Her heart gave its usual flutter. She loved to hear Willie whistle. It was to her a sure sign that her world was all in proper order. Willie rounded the wagon and his whistling stopped.

"Well, I'll be. Ya sure are up bright an' early this mornin'," he teased. "Mosquitoes drive ya out?"

Missie smiled. "Truth is, I didn't even notice 'em. My achin' joints were the first to tell me that it was time to do a little stretchin'. You feelin' a mite stiff, too?"

"Reckon I'd be lyin' iffen I didn't own up to feelin' a little sore here an' there," Willie said with a grin. "An' thet's all thet yer gonna git me to confess. Full-grown, able-bodied man shouldn't be admittin' to even thet. Folks will be thinkin' thet I never worked a day in my life."

Missie glanced at the well-muscled body of her husband. "Iffen they do," she said, "they sure got eyes that don't see much."

"Boy, I sure hurt," Henry put in. "Never realized how sore one's arms could git from drivin' horses, nor how much work it was to just sit on thet bumpin' ole wagon seat."

"We'll git used to it," Willie assured him, rolling a log over to sit on. "In a few days' time, we'll wonder why we ever felt it in the first place."

Willie asked God's blessing on the food and the day ahead, then Missie served out their breakfast.

After they had eaten, Henry left to check the other wagon. As

Missie washed up and packed away their supplies, Willie carefully went over his wagon and the harness. Many others were also moving about now. There were sounds of running and yelling children, barking dogs and calling mothers. Amid the early morning clamor, Missie heard a baby cry.

"Didn't know we had a baby along," she commented, watching Willie out of the corner of her eye.

"It's the Collins'," Willie responded. "Only 'bout seven months old."

"Quite a venture fer one so young."

"An' fer her young mama."

"This be her first?"

"No. She's got another one, too. Jest past two years old."

Missie thought for a moment.

"She'll have her hands full. Maybe the rest of us women can kinda give her a hand now an' then."

"I'm sure she'd 'preciate thet. There be another woman with the train who might need a hand now an' then as well."

Missie's head came up. "Someone not well?"

"Oh, I hope she's well enough—not fer me to know nor say; but she's expectin' a youngun."

"Oh."

Missie flushed slightly and hoped that Willie didn't notice.

"It jest could be thet it'll arrive somewhere along the trail. I talked to the wagon master and he says, 'No worry.' Claims lots of younguns are born on the way West. We have a midwife along, a Mrs. Kosensky. She's delivered a number of babies. Still, iffen it were *my* wife—"

"Iffen it were *your* wife?" Missie queried.

"Iffen it were my wife, I'd prefer thet she had a home to do the birthin' in—and a doc on hand, jest in case. In spite of Blake's bold words I still got the feelin' thet he was jest a mite edgy 'bout it all, an' would much prefer to have thet young mother safely into a town and under some doc's responsibility when her time is come."

"He can't be too worried," Missie said, "or he wouldn't have taken her on."

"From what I understand, the fact of the comin' baby wasn't told to Blake until all of the arrangements were made—an' then he jest hated to turn them down. They'd already sold their farm back east."

"Then Mr. Blake can't really be faulted, him not knowin'."

"Her man knew."

Missie turned away and busied herself in packing the coffee-pot and frying pan. "I'm sure she'll be fine. I'll look her up today. What's her name, by the way?"

"Her man's name is Clay. I think it be John Clay, but I'm not right sure 'bout thet."

"Have you seen her?"

"Jest offhand like. Their wagon is one of the first in line. I saw them last night when I was takin' the horses down for water. He was helpin' her down from the wagon. I don't think thet she was out much yesterday."

"She'll get the feel of it," Missie said, but she really wasn't as sure as she sounded. "Maybe she'll walk some today an' I'll get a chance to meet her."

One of the trail guides rode toward them on a rangy big roan with wild-looking eyes. He called out to each driver as he toured the circle, "Let's git those wagons hitched. Time to hit the trail."

Missie studied the big-boned horse, thinking that he looked like he could handle anything; yet she felt a thankfulness that she would never be called upon to ride him.

The men moved almost as one toward the tethered horses. The women hurried with their tasks of repacking each item into the wagons, putting out the fires and gathering their families to-gether. Missie's final tasks were already done so she stood beside her wagon and observed the bustling scene before her.

Again she heard the crying baby. She loved babies; still, she wasn't sure how wise or easy it would be to be heading West with one. She would see if she'd be able to give the young mother a hand.

Her thoughts then turned to the mother-to-be. Missie hoped that today she would be able to meet her. She hoped with all of her heart that all would go well for the young woman; but Willie's expressed concern wrapped itself about her like a restraining gar-ment. *I'll just have me a chat with Mrs. Kosensky*, she thought; *she's had experience birthing babies, and she'll know what to do.* Missie's concern evaporated like the morning mist.

Chapter 4

Traveling Neighbors

Missie made a special effort that day to get acquainted with her traveling companions. Mrs. Collins was not hard to find. Missie simply followed the sound of the crying baby. She located them a few wagons behind her own during the noon-hour break. Mrs. Collins was busy trying to prepare a midday meal for her hungry family. A small boy tugged at her skirt and the baby cried as the young mother jostled her on her hip.

Missie smiled and introduced herself.

"We've already finished eatin'," she said, "an' I was wonderin' iffen I could help with the baby whilst you got yer meal."

"Oh, would ya?" Mrs. Collins said with great relief in her voice. "I'd most appreciate it. Meggie's cryin' most drives me to distraction." She pushed the small boy from her. "Joey, please be patient. Mama will git yer dinner right away—jest you sit down an' wait."

The small boy plopped down on his bottom and began to cry, his voice loud and demanding.

Missie reached for the baby, whose crying seemed to gain

momentum at the sound of her brother, and walked back toward her own wagon. The poor mother would somehow have to cope with the howling Joey.

Missie walked back and forth, gently bouncing the baby and singing softly to her. The crying gradually subsided until only an occasional sob shook her tiny frame. Missie continued to rock and pace. When finally she checked the baby in her arms, she was sound asleep.

Missie returned to the mother who was now busy clearing away the dishes and pots, having fed her husband and son. *I hope that she took time to properly feed herself*, Missie thought.

Joey was sitting on a blanket, no longer crying in anger, although the smudge of tears and trail dust still smeared his cheeks. He looked very sleepy and Missie wondered how long it would be until he would be crying again.

"Thank ya—jest thank ya so much," Mrs. Collins said as she looked up from her task. "Ya can jest lay her down on the bed in the wagon."

Missie did so, having to move several items in order to find room for the tiny baby on the bed. She noticed that the Collins' living area was even smaller than the cramped quarters that she and Willie shared—and there were four Collinses.

Missie ducked out through the flap in the canvas.

"Looks like Joey should go to bed, too," she commented bravely.

"He's *so* tired," sighed the mother. Missie thought that she looked in need of a bed also.

"I'll tuck him in," offered Missie, wondering if Joey would allow himself to be tucked-in by a stranger.

To her surprise, he did not protest as she took his hand and helped him up. She started to lift him into the wagon, but stopped long enough to dip a corner of her apron in water and wash the tear-streaked face. His face was warm and flushed; Joey welcomed the temporary coolness of the wet apron.

Missie laid Joey on the bed, trying to keep him far enough away from Meggie that he wouldn't waken her. Even before Missie left the wagon, Joey's long eyelashes were fluttering in an attempt to fight off sleep. Sleep would soon win and the boy would get the needed rest that would improve his disposition. Perhaps when he awakened he would be easier for his young mother to cope with.

Missie left the wagon just as Mrs. Collins was stowing the last of her utensils. The wagons were about ready to move out.

"Why don't you crawl in an' catch a bit of rest with the children," Missie advised.

Mrs. Collins sighed deeply. "I think I will," she said, then turned to Missie. "I jest don't know how to thank ya." She blinked away tears. "Truth is, I was 'bout ready to give up."

"It'll get better," Missie promised, hoping sincerely that she was speaking the truth.

"Oh, I hope so—I truly hope so."

"We'll help."

"Thank ya." The young mother spoke with bowed head and moist eyes. "Yer very kind."

The call for "move-out" was yelled and Missie stepped aside.

"Best you get yourself settled," she said. "I'll see you later."

Mrs. Collins nodded, her weak smile trying valiantly to express her gratitude. She lifted herself wearily into her wagon. It was hot inside in the full heat of the day, but it was the most comfort that she would be able to find. She laid herself down between her sleeping children and let her tired body relax and rock with the swaying of the wagon.

Missie walked and rode intermittently. When she walked she chatted with the other women or children who happened to be near. She met Mrs. Standard, a gentle but firm-looking woman with a sturdy frame and graying hair; she had a family of eight—five girls and three boys. It was the second marriage for Mrs. Standard, a bride of seven months—and a mother for only the same period of time. She had had no children of her own from before, so the adjustment of caring for a brood of eight was a big one. She had always wanted a family, but to receive eight all at once—of various sizes, ages and temperaments—was an awesome task. Missie admired the woman for undertaking it with such gusto. Mrs. Standard had always been a "town girl" as well, so her marriage to the widower carried a double challenge. He was convinced that the rainbow's end must rest somewhere in the West, so Mrs. Standard had packed up his eight children, the few things of her own that she could find room for, and joined him in the long trek.

Mrs. Standard's usual walking companion was Mrs. Schmidt, a small, wiry woman who walked with a slight limp. She had three children—two nearly-grown sons and a girl of eight.

Neither of the two ladies talked much as they walked. Missie assumed that just giving orders to her large family was enough talking for Mrs. Standard, and Mrs. Schmidt didn't seem to have many thoughts that needed to be expressed. She was always busy *doing*, not talking. She gathered more firewood than she could ever manage to burn during the evening camping hours.

Missie learned the names of some of the other ladies as well. There was Mrs. Larkin, dark and unhappy looking, and Mrs. Page, who talked even faster than she walked—and she walked briskly. The women in the company had already been informed about every item that Mrs. Page possessed, as well as the cost to purchase it, and how it had been obtained. Missie would endure only short sessions near the woman, then drift further away, thankful for the excuse of picking up firewood.

Mrs. Thorne, a tall, sandy-haired woman, walked stiff and upright, striding ahead in the manner of a man. Her three children walked just like their mother, their arms swinging freely at their sides, their steps long and quick. Missie somehow felt that Mrs. Thorne would have no difficulty taking on the West.

A young woman who had waved to Missie on her first day on the trail she now discovered to be Kathy Weiss, who was traveling west with her widowed father. She had a sunny smile and an easygoing disposition. She seemed a dreamer, and at times Missie wondered if she realized where this journey was taking her, or if she just felt herself to be out for an afternoon stroll.

Already Kathy had made friends with the young-looking Mrs. Crane. She was a dainty, porcelain-doll type, who appeared to be in a state of shock over what was taking place. She was the train's display piece, refusing to dress herself in the common and rough, yet practical, cotton—the sensible thing to be wearing for this mode of travel and living. She wore, instead, fashionable dresses and bonnets and impractical, stylish shoes. Her grooming every morning took far more time than her breakfast preparations. Missie smiled at such vanity, but her heart went out to the girl.

Missie sought out Mrs. Kosensky, the midwife; she liked her immediately. The woman was a stoutish, motherly type, who found walking difficult. Her kind face and ready smile made Missie wish that she could somehow walk some of the miles for the older woman.

Missie saw other small groups of women and children here and there, changing and interchanging as the day wore on. She promised herself that she would make an effort to get to know each one of them as quickly as possible, so that she might take full advantage of friendships on the trail. She was impressed with the differences that existed among them. It seemed that since they had such a common purpose, they should somehow be more similar in background and personality.

All day long Missie watched for the expectant mother that Willie had spoken of. Missie was eager to meet the young Mrs. Clay, feeling a kinship with her, though her own secret would have to be guarded for a time. Though Missie sought out the other woman each time that she walked for a spell, she still had not spotted her when the teams were again called to an early halt. As she had the day before, Missie almost stumbled into camp, so weary was she from the day's long trek. She deposited her few sticks of firewood beside the wagon and went to speak with Willie.

As Willie's hands moved to unharness the team, Missie's eyes caught sight of swelling blisters where the reins had irritated the skin on his fingers. She mentioned them, but Willie shrugged it off.

"They'll soon toughen up," he said without concern. "Only takes a few days. How're you?"

"Tired—and sore. But I think that I'm farin' better than some of them. I noticed that Mrs. Crane was really limpin' when she climbed into her wagon back a piece."

"Is she the young peacock in the fancy feathers?"

Missie smiled. "Don't be too hard on her, Willie. She loves her nice things."

"Well, she'd be a lot wiser to pack 'em away fer awhile an' wear somethin' sensible."

"Maybe so, but she'll have to make up her own mind 'bout that."

"You'd best git some rest," Willie said, changing the subject as he prepared to move off with the horses. "Yer lookin' all done-in again."

Missie did rest, though this time she determined not to fall asleep. Instead, she settled herself against the wagon wheel, there being no big trees nearby, and worked on some knitting. She noticed that other women and children had settled themselves in the shade of the wagons and were finding some resting time as well. In fact, the only one bustling about was Mrs. Schmidt who was busily throwing more wood onto her already abundant pile.

The sounds of soft snoring drifted to Missie from the direction of the next wagon. She looked across to see Mrs. Thorne stretched out full length on the grass beside her wagon, one arm tucked beneath her head.

Mrs. Standard was busy across the way tending the stubbed toe of one of her step-children. He cried as she washed the injured foot; but he quieted after he realized what a fine conversation piece that neat white bandage made. He hobbled off to find someone who would rightfully appreciate his dreadful injury.

Another Standard youngster rolled on the ground with the family dog. Mrs. Standard moved away from the commotion and lowered herself to the ground with a heavy sigh. She removed her stout walking shoes and sat rubbing her feet. Missie could imagine how they ached, her own feet suffering in empathy.

It seemed to Missie that the time went too quickly. The sun moved further west and lost its fierceness. Gradually things in the camp began to stir. Mrs. Schmidt was the first to have a fire going, but then, she was going to need an early start if she was to burn up all that wood. Other fires were soon started and the smoke began to waft on the cooler air. Missie stirred herself and laid aside her knitting.

By the time Willie made his appearance the fire was burning

and the stew pot simmering. There was no need for Missie to make biscuits. Her mother's bread supply would last for a number of days yet, even though its freshness would be lost. Tonight it was still soft and tasty. Missie savored each bite.

Henry ate with a hearty appetite and Missie noticed that Willie wasn't far behind him in the amount of supper that he devoured.

"I been thinkin'," said Missie, "we should have brought along one cow that was milkin', 'stead of two that are months away from calvin'."

"Ya hankerin' fer some milk?"

"Coffee and tea suit me fine, but just look at all of the young-uns round about. They sure could do with some milk." Secretly, Missie realized that milk wouldn't be a bad idea for herself as well, but she said nothing about that fact.

Willie glanced over his many neighbors. There were a number of children, some of them very young.

"Yer right," he responded. "Seems to be younguns aplenty. Seen any more of Mrs. Collins since noon?"

"No. She must ride in the wagon most of the time. Who could walk with two babies to carry? I was thinkin' that maybe I'd slip over after we eat and see iffen she has some washin' that has to be done."

Willie frowned slightly. "Don't mind ya bein' neighborly, but are ya sure thet ya aren't pushin' a bit hard? Ya still look a little pale an' weary to me."

"Speakin' of bein' neighborly," Henry suddenly chimed as he laid his empty plate aside, "think I'll do a little visitin' myself." He rose to his feet with sudden enthusiasm, obviously suppressing a grin as he sauntered off.

"Oh, I'm fine," Missie quickly assured Willie. "A couple more days on the trail, an' I don't expect it'll bother me much atall."

Willie nodded a response of "I hope so," but the worried look did not leave his eyes.

"I still didn't see that Mrs. Clay," Missie went on. "I watched for her all day."

"I think she stayed pretty close to the wagon. I saw John—

that *is* his name—when I watered the horses. He says the sun has been a bit hard fer her to take.''

"Do you s'pose after we finish here we could walk over and see how they be?"

"Sure. Don't guess thet would be intrudin'." Willie reached for the Bible that he had placed on a stool nearby and again turned to the passage in Isaiah that Clark had marked.

"Fear thou not, for *I* am with thee," he read—then paused.

"What does thet mean to you, Missie?"

Missie looked serious as she thought about the words; then her eyes began to glow.

"I guess—" she said slowly, deliberately, "I guess that it means that God is right here with us by our campfire. O Willie! We need Him so much. Not just for the journey—the physical— but for the inner self, an' strength an'— I would be so lost without the Lord. It's hard enough leavin' Pa and Mama and the family—but, Willie, iffen I had to leave God behind too—I just couldn't go. I just couldn't. I'm so glad that He's comin' with us. So glad."

Willie's arm went around Missie's shoulder and drew her close. He worked on swallowing.

"Ya said what I'm a feelin', too," he spoke quietly. And when he was able to again control his voice, he led in a grateful prayer.

Chapter 5

Rebecca Clay

Missie cleared away the meal while Willie carried water from the little stream to refill their water barrel. The couple then set out to go and make the acquaintance of the Clays. It was a leisurely walk and many times they paused to talk with fellow travelers. Missie introduced Willie to the women and children that she had met; he in turn presented her to the men that he already knew.

When they passed the Collins' wagon, Missie stopped to ask if she could help with any washing. Mrs. Collins assured her that they were quite all right for at least another day. Missie was relieved, though she hoped that she didn't let it show. She would gladly have helped the young woman if the need had been there, but her own body was still sore and weary from her two days on the trail. Maybe by the morrow she would begin to feel more like herself.

Eventually they came to the Clay wagon. Willie greeted John and proudly introduced Missie. John, in turn, called for Rebecca who was busy inside the wagon. When she thought about it later, Missie wasn't sure how she had expected the young woman to look; but she was unprepared for the picture before her as Rebecca pushed back the flap of the canvas and descended slowly, reaching for her husband's hand to assist her. Her face looked tired and so very young; but a smile brightened her countenance as she saw Missie. The long auburn-brown hair was swept back from a pale face and held fast with a dark green ribbon. Her eyes held glints of green; Missie wondered if they changed color with her moods or with what she was wearing. Her smile came easily, generously—as though she were used to wearing it. Missie felt that she had never met a more appealing young woman. Rebecca was attractive—but it was more than that. Missie immediately found herself wanting to know her and become her friend.

As soon as Rebecca's feet were securely on the ground, she held out her hand to Missie.

"I'm Rebecca Clay." She spoke softly, controlled, "I'm so glad to meet you."

"An' I'm Melissa LaHaye," Missie responded. She wasn't sure why she had given her name as Melissa, but somehow she felt that this new friend should know who she *really* was. "Folks all just call me Missie," she added, not as an afterthought but more as an exchange of confidence.

"An' they call me Becky."

"That suits you," Missie said with a warm smile. She turned to Willie. "My husband Willie—he's met your John."

"Yes, John told me. I've been anxious to meet you both, but I've been a bit of a baby for the past two days. I hope that I'll soon be able to walk some with the rest of you. I'm sure that yer company would be much preferred over my own." She extended her hand. "Please, won't ya sit down. We have no soft chairs to offer, but those smooth rocks thet John rolled over aren't half bad."

Missie joined in with Becky's giggle as the four seated themselves on the rocks and settled in to talk. John replenished the fire in the hope of keeping away some of the hungry mosquitoes.

"An' jest where are you folks headin'?" Willie asked—the first question on all lips of those traveling West. Missie found herself hoping that the answer would bring good news of future neighboring.

"We travel with this train to Tettsford Junction, then rest for a few days before joinin' a group goin' northwest," John answered. "My brother went out last year an' sent word home thet ya never did see such good wheat land. He can hardly wait fer us to git there so thet he can show it off. Says ya don't even have to clear the land—jest put the plow to it."

Missie found that hard to believe, but others had told the same story. She felt disappointment as she realized that the Clays would not be her neighbors in the West after all.

"An' you?" John Clay asked.

"We catch the supply train headin' south when we git to Tettsford. I've got me some ranch land in the southern hills."

"Ya like thet country?"

"It's pretty as a dream. All hills an' sky an' grassy draws. Not much fer trees in the area. The little valley where I'm plannin' to build has a few trees, but nothin' like we have in the East."

"Understand thet there's no trees at all where we're headin'."

"I jest can't imagine country without trees," Becky said slowly.

Becky's voice sounded so wistful that Missie knew that she was going to sorely miss the trees. Missie felt a stirring in her own soul, but pushed it aside with a quick, "We'll get used to it."

Becky smiled. "I guess we will. Anyway, I s'pose I'll be too busy to notice much."

The men moved away to inspect John's harness. One section of the shoulder strap seemed to be rubbing a sore on his big black's right shoulder; John was anxious to find some way to correct the problem. As the men talked, Missie and Becky were left on their own.

"Did you leave a family behind?" Missie asked, thinking of her own parents.

"Jest my pa," answered Becky. "My mama died when I was fifteen."

"You don't look much more than fifteen now," Missie countered.

Becky laughed. "Everyone thinks I'm still a kid. Guess I jest look like one. Bet I'm every day as old as you—I'll be nineteen next October."

Missie was surprised. "Why you *are* most as old as me. When is your baby comin'?"

"In about two months. We're hopin' thet all goes well so thet we'll be in Tettsford Junction by then. They have a doctor there, you know."

"Really!" said Missie. "I didn't know the town was that big."

"Oh, it's quite an important place, really. Almost all of the wagon trains pass through it and then branch off in different directions."

"I sure do find me wishin' that you were comin' down our branch," Missie said with sincerity.

Becky looked at her frankly. "I feel the same way. It wouldn't be half so scary iffen I knew thet I'd have you for a neighbor, even iffen ya were near a day's ride away."

Both girls were silent for a few minutes. Missie toyed with the hem of her shawl while Becky poked without purpose at the fire.

"Missie," Becky spoke softly, "are you ever scared?"

Missie did not raise her eyes.

" 'Bout movin' West?"

"Yeah."

"I didn't *think* I was." Missie hesitated. "Willie was so excited, an' I honestly thought that I wanted to go too. An' I do, really I do. But I didn't know—that I'd—well—that I'd be such a baby, that it'd hurt so much to leave Mama an' Pa. I didn't think that I'd—well—feel so—empty." She stumbled over the words, and finally raised her head and said deliberately, "Well, yeah. Now I'm beginnin' to feel scared."

"I'm glad. I'm glad thet I'm not the only one, 'cause I feel like such a sissy. I've never told anyone, not even John. I want so much for him to have his dream, but—sometimes—sometimes I fear thet I won't be able to make it come true fer him, thet my homesickness will keep him from bein' really happy."

Missie's eyes widened.

"You feel homesickness?"

"Oh, yes."

"Even without leavin' behind a ma?"

"Maybe even more so. My pa loved my mama so much thet it was powerful hard on him when he lost her. I was all he had, an'—when John came along, I—well—I fell so in love thet I couldn't think of anyone else. So I've—I've left Pa—all alone.''

Becky's eyes filled with tears. She brushed them away and continued, ''If only he still had Mama I wouldn't worry 'bout him so much. I miss him—so very much. He's such a good man, Missie, so strong in the physical sense—big, muscular, tough. But inside, deep inside, so helpless. He's so tender, so—so—touched. . . . Do ya understand what I mean?''

Now it was Missie's eyes that filled with tears. She nodded. '' 'Deed I do. I know just such a man, an' I wouldn't be one bit surprised that he's cryin' silent tears for me just as often as I'm weepin' for him.''

''So yer lonesome, too?''

A quiet nod was her answer.

''I expect it gits better.''

''I hope so. I truly hope so,'' Missie said fervently. ''I'm countin' on God to make it so.''

''You know God?''

''Oh, yes, without Him—''

''I'm so glad! Becky exclaimed. ''It's Him thet gives me daily courage, too. I'm not very brave—even *with* Him; but *without* Him I'd be a downright coward.''

Missie sniffed away her tears and laughed at Becky's confession.

''I'm glad I've got Willie. He has enough courage for the both of us.''

''So does John. He can see nothin' but good in our future. Oh, I do hope that I won't let him down.''

Missie reached over and squeezed the girl's hand. ''You won't,'' she said firmly. ''You've got more courage than you 'llow yourself, or you wouldn't be here.''

''Oh, Missie, I hope so.''

''Are you afraid—'bout the baby?''

''A little. But I try not to think 'bout things like thet. Mostly I'm jest tired an' a little sick from the sun an' the motion of the wagon. I'll be so glad when I'm feelin' well enough to walk.''

''You must be careful not to walk too far at first.''

''John thinks thet walkin' will do me a powerful lot of good.

He says thet fresh air an' good exercise is all I need. His ma had nine babies an' never missed a day's work with any of 'em.''

Well, 'rah for John's ma, Missie wanted to say, but she bit her tongue. Instead she said, "There's a midwife here. She's delivered lots of babies. She'll tell you iffen you should be pushin' yourself for walkin'.''

"John told me thet there was a woman here, but I haven't met her yet.''

"You'll like her; I met her today. She's just the kind of woman that one would like to help with a birthin'. I'll bring her 'round, iffen you'd like.''

"Would you, Missie? I haven't felt up to seekin' her out, an' I do have a lot of questions. Iffen my mama. . . .'' Becky did not finish but brushed away some more tears.

"I'll bring her 'round tomorrow, iffen I can,'' Missie assured her gently.

Missie continued, "When we left—Willie an' me—my pa gave us a special verse. We kinda claim it as ours, but no one has *special* claim on God. His promises are for all of His children. I'd like to share our verse with you. I hope it will be as special to you as it is to Willie an' me. It comes from Isaiah an' it goes like this: 'Fear thou not; for I am with thee: be not dismayed; for I am thy God: I will strengthen thee; yea, I will help thee; yea, I will uphold thee with the right hand of my righteousness.' That's an awful lot of promise for one verse to offer, but I feel sure that God really means it. He can—and will—be with us, in life or in death—in just *everything.*''

"Thank you, Missie, I really needed thet. When you drop by on the morrow, would ya do something fer me? It's too dark to see proper-like right now, but I'd like ya to show me where thet verse is so thet I can read it over an' over. Would ya do thet?''

"I'd be glad to.''

The menfolk had gone on down to check the horses and to rub some of Willie's ointment on the black's shoulder. The silence that followed Missie's words was broken only by the crackling of the fire. Missie found herself wishing that she could tell Becky her own good news, but she held it back. Willie must be the first one to know. She must tell Willie—soon. It wasn't right to keep it from him. If only he wouldn't worry so. If she could just conquer her tiredness and perk up a bit. How thankful she was that she hadn't been troubled with bouts of morning sickness.

Becky interrupted her thoughts. "I'm afraid thet I have to confess to a lie, Missie. I *am* scared—'bout the baby, 'bout maybe not havin' a doctor, 'bout the way thet I've been feelin'. I don't know one thing 'bout babies, Missie—not 'bout their birthin' nor their care. The thought of maybe havin' thet baby on this trip west nigh scares me to death, but John says. . . ." She shook her head slowly and let the words hang.

Missie spoke quickly. "An' John's right. That baby will prob-'ly be born in Tettsford in a pretty bedroom with a doc there to fuss over him. But iffen—iffen he does decide to hurry it up a bit, then we have Mrs. Kosensky—'bout as good a woman as you'd find anywhere. Just you wait 'til you get to know her. She'll put your mind at ease. I'll fetch her 'round, first chance I get."

Becky summoned a smile. "Thanks, Missie. Boy, you must think a real crybaby, carryin' on so over an ordinary happen-in' like a baby's comin'. I'd like to meet Mrs. Ko—Ko—what's her name? Maybe she can even git me feelin' better so thet I can do some walkin' with ya. I feel like every bone in my body has been reduced to mush by thet jarrin', bouncin' wagon." She smiled and rose. "The men should be comin' back soon. Do ya thing they'd like some coffee?"

Chapter 6

On the Trail

On Saturday night after supper, Mr. Blake called for a gathering of the members of the wagon train.

"Life on a trek west can be rather dull," he stated matter-of-factly, "so iffen any of ya can play anything thet makes a squeak, we'd 'preciate it iffen you'd bring it out."

It was discovered that Henry played a guitar and Mr. Weiss a rather beat-up-looking fiddle. A sing-song 'round the fire was called for and folks joined in heartily, humming the tunes when they did not know the words. Some of the children jumped or skipped or swayed to the tunes in their own version of a folk dance.

It was surprising what Mr. Weiss could accomplish on his worn-out fiddle, and Henry was quite adept in keeping up with him. Henry also possessed a pleasant singing voice and led the group in one song after another. Missie enjoyed it; she decided that Henry was well worth feeding and determined to always be ready with a generous second filling of his plate.

Mr. Blake stood far too soon and waved his hand for attention.

"Thank ya, men—thank ya. You've done a fine job. Now it's gittin' late and time to be turnin' in. 'Sides, the mosquitoes are 'bout as hungry as I've ever see'd 'em." He waved a few away from his face.

"Tomorrow, bein' Sunday, the train will stay to camp. Me, I'm not a religious man, but a day of rest jest plain makes sense—fer the animals an' fer us people. Now iffen you who are religious are hankerin' fer some kind of church service, I'm leavin' ya on yer own to do the plannin'. I'm no good at sech things. Fact is, I plan on spendin' tomorrow down at yonder crik, seein' iffen I can catch me some fish.

"Now, then, be there any of you who be wantin' church?"

Quite a few hands were raised.

"Fine—fine," Mr. Blake said. "Klein, ya figurin' thet you can take charge?"

Henry nodded his assent and the meeting was dismissed.

Henry spent some time calling upon his wagon neighbors in preparation for the morrow's service. A few did not wish to take part, but most were eager to worship on the Lord's day.

Willie was appointed to read the Scripture; Henry himself took charge of the singing. And it was found that Mr. Weiss could play hymns on his old violin with even more feeling than he played the lively dance tunes and folk songs.

Sunday dawned clear and warm. The service had been set for 9:00 so that it would be over before the sun hung too hot in the sky. The people gathered in a grove of trees near the stream and settled themselves beneath the protective branches on logs that Willie and Henry had cut and placed there for that purpose.

They began with a hearty hymn-sing, Henry leading in a clear baritone voice. Kathy Weiss taught the group a new song—simple and short but with a catchy tune. Many hands clapped in accompaniment when they were not occupied elsewhere slapping mosquitoes.

Henry finally called a halt to the singing and asked Mr. Weiss to lead the group in prayer. He did, with such fervor that Missie was reminded of home.

Anyone who wished was invited to tell of their experiences on the trail. One by one, many stood expressing thanks to God for

His leading, for strength, for assurance in spite of fears, for incidents of protection along the way. Missie and Becky exchanged looks of confidence and meaningful smiles.

After the last voluntary speaker had sat down, Willie read the Scripture. The people listened attentively as Willie's voice carried to them his excitement over the promises of God. When he closed the book there were many "amens."

It had been a good service, and as the people left they shook Henry's hand and thanked him for a job well done. Some suggested another hymn-sing round the fire that night, and so it was arranged.

The Sunday service and Sunday night hymn-sing became even more popular with the wagon-train members than the Saturday night doings. As the weeks went by, some of those who had not been interested at first in joining the Sunday crowd for their worship time found themselves washing their faces, putting on clean clothes, brushing the trail dust off their boots and heading for whatever spot had been set aside for that week's service. Missie and Willie were pleased to see the interest grow. The folks appeared to really need that restful time of worship and sharing on Sunday.

Mr. Blake, in the meantime, was left to his own choice of Sunday activity, whether it was hunting, fishing or just lying in the shade. Missie noticed him on one particular Sunday morning, though, when he had chosen to just loaf around camp. It looked suspiciously as if he were listening.

Chapter 7

Tedious Journey

Day after long day rolled and bounced slowly by. Even the weather became monotonous. The sun blazed down upon them daily with only an occasional shower to bring temporary relief.

But gradually the travelers adjusted to the journey. Bodies still ached at the end of the day, but not with the same intense painfulness. Blisters had been replaced by callouses. Some of the horses had become lame; drivers watched with concern for any serious signs of injury to their animals.

One family, the Wilburs, had been forced to pull aside and retire from the train due to a lame horse that just could not continue on. Mr. Blake detoured the train about two miles out of its way in order to drop the young couple off at a small army outpost. The sergeant in charge said that he'd send a few of his men back with Mr. Wilbur to retrieve his stranded wagon and lead the horses to the safety of the fort. At the earliest future date the Wilburs would be escorted to the nearest town. Missie could have wept when she saw the look of intense disappointment—the look of living pain—that the couple wore as the train moved on without them.

Then there had been some minor mishaps. One of the Page children had received burns from playing too near a cooking fire; Mr. Weiss, the train's blacksmith, had been kicked by a horse he was attempting to shoe; Mrs. Crane had twisted her ankle badly as she scaled a steep hill in her high-fashion shoes; and a few of the young children were plagued with infected mosquito bites. But, all in all, everyone had adjusted quite well to life on the trail.

The countryside began changing. Missie tried to determine just what it was that made it seem so different—foreign—but it was hard to define. The trees were smaller and different than most of the trees that she had been|used to. The hills appeared different, too. Perhaps it was the abundance of short growth that clung to the sides of them. Whatever the difference, Missie realized that she was getting farther and farther away from her old home and those that she loved. The now-familiar feeling of lonesomeness sometimes gnawed and twisted within her. Once in a while she was forced to bite her lip to keep the ready tears from spilling down her cheeks. She must try harder, pray more; and as she walked or worked she repeated over and over to herself the blessed promise of Isaiah. Her greatest ally was busyness, and she tried hard to keep her hands and her mind occupied.

Missie visited Becky often, keeping her promise of introducing her to the midwife, Mrs. Kosensky. Mrs. Kosensky had vetoed John's advice that Becky walk more and cautioned her to be careful about her amount of activity each day. Becky chafed under the restrictions but obeyed the new orders.

Missie also found plenty of opportunity to help Mrs. Collins in the care of her two young children. She often took the baby girl to visit Becky so that Becky might have some experience in the handling of a baby.

Try as she might to keep her thoughts on the adventure ahead, Missie found that she was continually recalling the events of the day as they would be taking place "back home." *Today Mama will be hanging out the wash, all white and shimmerin' in the sun;* or *today Pa will be makin' his weekly trip into town.* Or on Sunday, *the whole family is in the buggy and headin' for the little log church where they will meet and worship with their neighbors and Parson Joe.* Her dear Clae's Joe would bring the sermon that would be Amen'ed by all of the people.

And so Missie went through each day; her weary but toughening body traveled with the other pilgrims of the wagon train but her spirit soared "back home" where she shared the days' activities with those that she had left behind.

With surprise one day she realized as she prepared the evening meal that they had been on the trail for almost four weeks. In some ways it had seemed forever; and in others, it seemed not so long at all. But if it had been so long, why hadn't some of her hurting stopped? Time, she had thought, would lessen the pain, erase the burden of loneliness. How much time was required before one began to feel a whole person again?

As Missie's body ached less, it seemed that her spirit ached more. How she missed them—each one of them. How good it would be to feel her mama's warm embrace, or her pa's hand upon her shoulder. How she would welcome the teasing of Clare and Arnie or enjoy watching the growing-up of her younger sister, Ellie. And little Luke in his soft lovableness—how she ached to hug him again. "Oh, dear God," she prayed again and again, "please make me able to bear it."

With all of her strength, Missie fought to keep her feelings from Willie; but in so doing she didn't realize how much of her true self she was withholding from him. She often felt Willie's eyes upon her, studying her face. He fretted over her weariness and continually checked to be sure that she was feeling all right, was not overworking, was eating properly.

The truth was, Missie was not feeling well. Apart from her deep homesickness, there was nausea and general tiredness. But she didn't admit it to Willie. *It's not the right time yet. Willie would just worry,* she kept telling herself. But she sensed—and did not like—the strain that was present between them.

Each day became very much like the others. The LaHayes always rose early. Missie prepared breakfast for Willie and Henry while they checked and watered the animals and prepared them for the new day's travel. They ate, packed up and moved out. At noon they took a short break and Missie again prepared a simple meal.

When they stopped at the end of the day, there was the fire to start, the meal to be cooked and the cleaning up to be done. Very little fresh food now remained, so Missie began resorting to dried and home-canned foods. She was fast wearying of the limited menu over and over. She wondered if it was as distasteful to Willie and Henry as it was to her. What wouldn't she give to be able to sit down to one of her mother's appetizing meals?

The amount of walking Missie did depended on the terrain and the intensity of the heat. Becky Clay did not attempt to walk far each day. John kindly refrained from prodding her to do more than she felt comfortable doing, coming to the realization that all women were not as hardy as his mother. Becky did welcome time with the other ladies, even though she had to be careful not to overdo.

The travelers began to know one another as individuals, not just faces. For some, this was good. Mrs. Standard and Mrs. Schmidt seemed to accept and enjoy one another more each day. They hoped to be close neighbors when the journey ended.

Kathy Weiss and Tillie Crane also became close friends, though Kathy also spent many hours with Anna, the oldest of the five Standard girls. Anna and Tillie shared no common interest, however, and seemed to have no desire to spend time in one another's company. In turn, Mrs. Standard seemed to enjoy Kathy and embraced her right along with her own recently acquired brood of eight. Missie imagined that Mrs. Standard would have been willing to take in almost anybody.

Henry, too, seemed to be a welcome visitor around the Standard campfire. Missie often wondered if the attraction for him was one of the young girls, or the motherly Mrs. Standard— Henry was not able to remember his own mother who had died when he was young.

As well as fast friendships among the travelers, there were also a few frictions. Mrs. Thorne still carried herself stiff and straight, never making an effort to seek out anyone's company, or with word or action to invite anyone to share any time with her. There were no neighborly visits over a coffee cup around the Thornes' fire.

Everyone seemed to avoid the chattering of Mrs. Page; but she had a way of popping up out of nowhere and making it virtually impossible for one to escape without being downright rude. She would have cozied up to a cactus if she had thought that it had ears—yet even Mrs. Page was not willing to share her goodwill with everyone.

Missie never did know what had started it in the first place, but for some reason a deep animosity had grown between Mrs. Page and Mrs. Tuttle. Mrs. Tuttle was a widow, traveling west with her brother. Unlike Mrs. Page, she had very little to say, but what words she used were often acidic.

Mrs. Page had too much to say and she enjoyed elaborating on any subject—including the reason for which Mrs. Tuttle was going west. According to Mrs. Page, a trapper was waiting at the other end of the trail, having made a sort-of proposal by mail. Mrs. Page was sure that the trapper was "trapped"; that if he'd been able to get a good look at Mrs. Tuttle's stern face, he would have preferred a wolverine. So the war waged on.

Most of the battles between them were fought via messengers. "You tell Jessie Tuttle thet iffen she doesn't learn how to crack the ice on thet face of hern, she'll lose thet trapper as soon as she finds 'im."

"You tell Mrs. Page [Jessie Tuttle would not allow herself to use Mrs. Page's first name, Alice] that when she cracked the ice off her own face she did a poor job of it. Now the button fer her mouth don't hold it shut none."

Of course the messengers never did deliver the messages, but it wasn't necessary for them to do so. The insults were always spoken loudly within earshot of the party that they were intended for. The running battle provided no alarm and a small measure of amusement for the other members of the wagon train. There was little enough to smile at, so even a neighborly squabble was welcomed.

Occasionally a meeting of all adult members of the train was called. There, the wagon master gave up-to-date reports on progress, or issued a new order, or explained some new situation. Even such a meeting was looked upon as relief from the usual.

Again Mr. Blake called a meeting. He told them he was

pleased at the progress made. They were right on schedule. His first concern was the large river that would soon need to be crossed; if conditions remained as they were, they would reach the ford in four days' time. He was sure that the river would be down, making the crossing an easy one. Heavy rains were the only obstacle that would sometimes hamper the crossing, Mr. Blake said, and they had been particularly blessed with sunny, clear days. Once across the Big River, as it was called by the local Indians, they were well on their way.

Everyone seemed to rejoice at Mr. Blake's news, but deep down inside, Missie knew that she did not. Within her was a secret wish that the river would not be fordable and that Willie would decide to turn around and go back home.

Willie did not share her wish. At the wagon master's encouraging announcement, he had cheered as loudly as any of the travelers. Only a few of the womenfolk had remained silent; Missie, Becky, Sissie Collins and Tillie Crane were among them.

Missie was quiet on the way back to the wagon, but Willie was too excited to notice.

"Jest think," he enthused, "only four more days an' we cross the Big River, an' then—then we'll *really* start to roll!"

Missie nodded and tried to coax forth a smile for Willie's sake.

"Are ya still worryin' 'bout Becky?" Willie queried, seeking some reason for Missie's restraint.

"Sorta," Missie responded, feeling that the answer was both safe and, in a measure, truthful.

"But there's something else, too—isn't there? I've been feelin' it fer a long time. Aren't ya feelin' well, Missie?"

It was asked with such concern that Missie knew somehow she must attempt to put Willie's mind at ease. This wasn't the way that she would have chosen to break the news to Willie. She had pictured the closeness of their shared bed, or the intimacy of their own fireside; and here they were walking over a rutted, dusty path, with people before, behind and beside them. There seemed almost no way for her to speak low enough so that she wouldn't be heard by others. Yet she knew that she must speak.

"I been wantin' to tell you, but the time never seemed right," she said quietly. She took a long breath. "Willie—we're gonna have a baby, too."

Willie stopped walking and reached for Missie. His face was very sober.

"Ya aren't joshin'?"

"No, Willie."

"An' yer sure?"

"Quite sure."

Willie stood silently for a moment, then shook his head. "I'm not sure thet wagon-trainin' an' babies go together."

For a brief minute Missie hoped that maybe this would give Willie a reason to head for home, but she quickly pushed the selfish thought from her and managed a smile.

"Oh, Willie, don't fuss. We'll be in our own place long before our baby ever arrives."

"Ya sure?"

"Of course. How long you think we're gonna be on this trail, anyway?"

The look on Willie's face suddenly changed and he let out a whoop. Missie reached out to hush him before he shouted his news to the whole wagon train. Willie stopped whooping and hugged Missie tightly. Relief flooded over her. He was excited about it—there was no doubting it.

Suddenly Missie wanted to cry. She wasn't sure why, but it was such a joy to tell her news to Willie, to see his exuberance and to feel his strong arms about her. She had been wrong to withhold it from him. A great wave of love for Willie washed over her; at the moment she would have gone to the end of the earth with him if he had wanted her to.

They laughed and cried together as Willie held her in his arms and kissed her forehead and her hair. Their fellow travelers had passed on by them and returned to their campfires.

When Willie could speak again, he stumbled over his words, trying to say so much, all at one time.

"So this is why ya haven't been yerself. We gotta take better care of ya. Ya need more rest an' a better diet. I'll have to git fresh meat oftener. Ya shouldn't be doin' so much. Ya'll overdo. I was so scared, Missie, thet maybe you'd changed yer mind, thet ya didn't want to go out West—or thet maybe ya didn't even love me anymore—or thet ya had some bad sickness—or—oh, I was scared. I jest prayed an' prayed an' here—here. . . ."

Missie had not realized what her long days of listlessness and homesickness had put Willie through. She must not hold back from him again.

"I'm sorry, Willie," she whispered, "I didn't know that you were feelin'—were thinkin' all those things. I'm sorry."

"Not yer fault. Not yer fault at all. I'm jest so relieved, thet's all. Still sorry thet yer not feelin' well—but we'll take care of ya. After all, it be fer a *very* good reason!"

"I'm glad that you're happy—" but Missie didn't get a chance to finish her sentence. Willie stopped her as he drew her close.

"Everything is gonna be fine now, Missie. Ya should be feelin' better soon. We'll have a chat with Mrs. Kosensky. We'll make sure thet ya git lots of rest. An' 'fore ya know it, you'll be fine, jest fine."

"Willie? Willie, there's somethin' else, too. True, I've been feelin' a mite down. But I think the true reason for me—my— ah— well, the way I feel is—just lonesomeness, Willie. Just lonesomeness for Mama an' Pa an'. . . ." Missie could not continue. The tears ran freely.

Willie pulled her close against him. He stroked her hair and gently wiped the tears from her cheek.

"Why didn't ya tell me, Missie?" he said at last. "I woulda' understood. I been missing those left behind, too. Maybe I couldn't have eased yer sorrow none, Missie, but I'd a shared it with ya." He tipped her face and gently kissed her. "I love ya, Missie."

Why had she been so foolish? Why had she hugged her hurt to herself, thinking that Willie would not understand or care? She should have told him long ago and accepted the comfort of his arms. Missie clung to him now and cried until her tears were all spent. Surely there was some healing in shared heartache, in cleansing tears. At length she was able to look up at Willie and smile again.

Willie kissed her on the nose and gave her another squeeze.

"Hey," he said suddenly, "we gotta git this little mama off to bed. No more late nights fer you, Missus. An' not quite so much walkin' an' doin', either."

"Oh, Willie," protested Missie, "the walkin' is a heap easier for me than that bumpy ol' wagon."

"Ya reckon so?"

"I reckon so. It's not exactly a high-springed buggy, you know."

Willie chuckled as he led Missie carefully across the clearing to their wagon.

"Mind yer step, now," he said earnestly as he boosted her up.

"Oh, Willie," Missie laughed in exasperation. But she knew that she was in for a lot of babying in the future. Well, maybe it wouldn't be so bad if he just wouldn't overdo it. She smiled to herself and ducked to enter through their canvas doorway.

Chapter 8

Rain

The next morning Willie was still in his state of happiness as he awoke to begin a new day.

He pulled his gray, woolen shirt over his head and did up the buttons from waist to neck, then tucked it into his coarse denim pants. He promised himself that if the day again got too hot, he'd change the shirt for a cotton one. He raised his suspenders and eased them over his shoulders, snapping them into place. At the entrance to the wagon he stopped and pulled on his calf-high leather boots. As he shrugged his way out of the canvas doorway and headed out to get the team ready for the day's journey, he went with an even jauntier step and cheerier whistle than usual. Missie knew that he was pleased about the coming baby. She also knew that he was thinking, *four more days to the Big River!* To Missie, it meant four more days to the point of no return.

She tried to shake off the melancholy for Willie's sake and went about her morning chores with a determined cheerfulness. Today, if she had the opportunity, she *might* reveal the good news of her coming baby to Becky. They could plan together.

Willie stopped the team often that morning to give Missie breaks for walking—and then to check that she hadn't already walked far enough. She humored him by walking for awhile and then welcoming a ride when he suggested it. She actually could have walked for almost the entire morning. The walking bothered her less each day, but there was no use worrying Willie.

In the afternoon, dark storm clouds appeared and the whole wagon train seemed to be holding its breath in unison. It was soon apparent that this storm would not pass over with just a shower. Still, the team drivers and their apprehensive womenfolk entertained the hope that the rain would not last for long. The animals seemed to sense the approaching storm too, and by the time the thunder and lightning commenced, they were already tense.

The rain came lightly at first. The women and children scrambled for cover, but the men wrapped themselves in canvas slickers and drove on through the storm.

As the day wore on, the intensity of the storm increased. The dark clouds overhead seemed angry and invective as they poured down their waters from a sodden sky. Soon the teams were straining to pull the heavy, high-wheeled wagons through the deepening mud. Those fortunate enough to have extra horses or oxen hitched them also to their vehicles.

The wagon train guides ranged back and forth, watching for trouble along the trail. It came all too soon. One of the lead wagons slid while going down a slippery, steep slope and bounced a wheel against a large rock. The wooden spokes snapped with a sickening sharpness. The wagon lurched and heaved but did not tip over. Mr. Calley somehow kept the startled horses from bolting.

The teams following had to maneuver around the crippled wagon, slipping and sliding their way down the rocky hill and onto even ground. As soon as the last wagon was safely down the badly rutted hillside, Mr. Blake ordered a halt. They should have done many more miles of traveling before stopping, but it was useless to try to go on. The Big River would have to wait.

The wagons gathered into their familiar circular formation and the teams were unhitched. Some of the men went back up the hill to help the unfortunate Calley family. Their wagon could not be moved until the broken wheel was mended. The men labored in the cold rain, trying to raise the corner of the wagon piling rocks and pieces of timber underneath to level it. The Calleys would have to spend the night in it, in spite of its location.

While Willie and Henry were gone, Missie wrapped a heavy shawl tightly about her and went in search of firewood. The other ladies and children were seeking dry material for their fires as well, and there was very little to be found. Missie felt cold and muddy and cross as she scrambled for bits and pieces of anything that she thought might burn. At one point she heard a commotion and then a hoarse voice shouting, "You tell Jessie Tuttle thet once a body is headin' fer a stick of firewood, thet body is entitled to it." Missie smiled in spite of herself. They were at it again!

Only Mrs. Schmidt did not have to join the searchers. Her ever-abundant supply of dry wood was unloaded from under the wagon seat. Missie wondered why she hadn't had the presence of mind to plan ahead as well.

Missie finally had what she hoped would be enough to cook a hot meal, then sloshed her way back through the wetness to her wagon. The fire was reluctant, at best, but Missie finally coaxed a flame to life. It sputtered and spit and threatened to go out, but Missie encouraged it on. The coffee never did boil, but the reheated stew was at least warm, and the near-hot coffee was welcome to shivering bodies.

Missie cleaned up in a quick, half-hearted manner, with Willie's help, and they crawled into their canvas home to get out of their wet clothing and into something warm and dry. It was far too early to go to bed, even though the day had been a strenuous one. Willie lit a lamp and settled down beside it to bring his journal up-to-date. Missie picked up her knitting, but her fingers were still too cold to work effectively. At length she gave up and pulled a blanket around herself for warmth. Willie stirred, noticed her shivering, and started fretting again.

"Ya chilled? Ya'd best git right into thet bed—don't want ya pickin' up a cold. Here, let me help ya. I'll go see what I can find for a warm stone fer yer feet." He bundled Missie up, right to the chin and reached for his coat.

"Don't go back out in the rain—please, Willie. My feet aren't that cold. They'll be warm in no time. I'll just slip on a pair of your woolen socks." And Missie did so immediately so that Willie could see that she meant what she said.

It was too early to go to sleep, Missie knew. She also knew that it was unwise to protest being tucked in, so she snuggled under the blanket and gradually the chill began to leave her bones. She even began to feel drowsy.

Willie finished his journal entries and picked up a leather-covered edition of *Pilgrim's Progress* which had been a wedding gift from Missie's school children. Missie murmured, "Iffen you don't mind, would you read aloud?"

Willie read and the long evening somehow passed by.

The rain continued to fall, splattering against the canvas of the wagon. Before laying himself down to sleep, Willie checked carefully all around the inside of their small dwelling to make sure that there were no leaks. He then crawled in beside Missie and pulled the warm covers close about himself. In a very few minutes Missie knew by his breathing that he slept. She wished that she could fall asleep as easily, but she instead lay and listened to the rain. Again her thoughts turned to home.

She used to love to listen to the rain pattering on the window as she snuggled down beneath the warm quilt her mama had made. The rain had always seemed friendly then, but somehow tonight it did not seem to be a friend at all. She shivered and moved closer to Willie. She was thankful for his nearness and his warmth.

Chapter 9

Delays

When Missie awakened the next morning, the rain was still falling. Puddles of water lay everywhere. Shrubbery and wagons dripped steady little streams in the soggy morning air. Willie arrived just as Missie was about to crawl down from the wagon; she was wondering what in the world she would ever do about a fire. Ordering her to stay where she was, he managed to get a fire going and make some coffee and pancakes. He served Missie in the covered wagon, ignoring her protests.

"No use us both gittin' wet," he reasoned. " 'Sides Mr. Blake hasn't decided yet whether we move on or jest sit tight."

But Mr. Blake was concerned about reaching the Big River before the waters were swollen with the rain. So in spite of the mud, he ordered them to go on as usual.

Willie was already wet as he climbed up onto the wagon seat and urged the balking horses out.

It was tough going. The wagons slipped and twisted through the mire. Wheels clogged up and had to be freed from their burdens of mud. Teams and drivers were worn out in two hours' time. When one poor horse finally fell and needed a great deal of assistance regaining his footing, an order was called to halt. It was useless to try to travel under such conditions.

Missie didn't know whether to feel relief or dismay when the wagon creaked to a stop. The rain had slackened somewhat, so she wrapped her heavy, woolen shawl closely about her and went in the inevitable search for firewood. But when Willie returned sometime later, Missie still had not succeeded in getting a fire going. She was close to tears and felt like a complete failure. The wood just would not burn. Willie took charge, chasing Missie into the wagon to change her wet clothes; he dared to beg some hot water from Mrs. Schmidt whose fire was burning cheerily, seeming to stick its tongue out at the whole camp. Mrs. Schmidt was pleased to share her hot water—though a bit smug. Missie made tea in the confines of the wagon and she, Willie and Henry enjoyed the hot refreshment with their cold biscuits.

Still the rain continued. Missie knitted while Willie mended a piece of harness. When that was done, he pulled out his journal; but this source of activity was soon exhausted as well. He picked up the John Bunyan volume again and attempted to read, but eventually his restlessness drove him from the wagon and out into the rain, muttering an excuse about checking on the teams and the cows.

With Willie gone, the time dragged even more for Missie. She was just on the verge of venturing forth herself when Willie returned. At his call from the back of the wagon, Missie raised the tent flap. He handed her a bundle; it was the Collins' baby.

"Their wagon is leakin'," he explained. "There ain't a dry place to lay the younguns. I'll be right back with the boy."

Missie busied herself with unbundling the baby. True to his word, Willie was soon back with Joey. Meggie fussed and Missie gladly spent her time hushing her, rocking her back and forth and coaxing her to settle into a comfortable position. Willie entertained Joey, helping him to make a cabin with small sticks. Then he read to him out of *Pilgrim's Progress,* and even though much of the story the young boy could not possibly understand, he listened intently. Missie finally managed to get the baby to sleep. She joined Willie and Joey now involved in a little-boy game.

Sissie Collins dropped by later to check on her children and nurse the baby. Willie again made the rounds of the camp to see if there was anyone else needing a helping hand.

When the long day came to an end, they drank the remains of the now cold tea, and ate some cold meat with their biscuits.

Willie moved into the other wagon with Henry and let Sissie and her two little ones stay with Missie.

As Missie went to sleep again with the sound of the rain on the canvas roof, she wondered if it would never stop. How could they ever endure another day such as this had been?

But they did. Somehow. Day after day. At times the rain slackened to a mere drizzle and at other times it poured. Each time that the rain slowed its pace, Missie pulled her shawl tightly about her and left the confines of the wagon—but actually there was no place to go. The ground looked like a lake with only a few high spots still showing through. At first Missie tried to keep to the high ground; then giving up with a shrug, she sloshed through the water.

Finally even Mrs. Schmidt ran out of firewood, so the men made a combined effort to find something that would burn. Eventually it was decreed that one fire, built under a stretched-out canvas, would be shared by the whole camp. The women came by turns, three or four at a time, to hastily prepare something hot for their families.

The Collinses weren't the only ones having problems with leaking canvas. Other wagons, too, were wet—inside and out; families were doubling up and sharing quarters wherever possible.

The rain heightened the tension between the two antagonists; but the howls of outrage from Mrs. Page and the biting retorts of Mrs. Tuttle were often the very thing that kept the rest of the company sane. It was a nice diversion to be able to laugh—even at one another.

On the fifth day the sky began to clear, and the sun broke through on the dripping and miserable wagon train.

The people, too, came out, stringing lines and hanging clothing and blankets to dry. The ground remained soggy. It could be days before the stands of water disappeared and even a longer time before the ground would be dry enough to allow the wagons to roll.

Missie felt somewhat like Noah as she descended from her wagon. There was water everywhere. How good it would be to see the dry land appear and the horses kick up dust again. Oh, to be on the move again!

Mr. Blake felt impatient, too, but his many years on the trail told him that it would be useless to try to travel on in the mud. No, they'd have to wait. Mr. Blake also knew that with the rains of the past few days the Big River would be impossible to cross very soon. But there was no need to pass this information on to the group. They'd take the problems one day at a time.

Chapter 10

The Big River

For six days Mr. Blake kept the wagons in the camp. He would have held them longer, because he knew the unwelcome surprise that probably awaited them at the Big River, but he sensed the growing impatience to be rolling again. The ground in the immediate vicinity was dry enough to travel and the people were beginning to get restless. He did not want to risk trouble developing from tense nerves and idle hands, so he reluctantly called for the travelers to break camp.

Nonetheless, the six days had not been lost in inactivity. Harnesses had been repaired, wagons reinforced, canvases carefully patched and oiled where the relentless rain had found a way in. Clothes were washed and mended, blankets aired and bodies scrubbed. A hunting party had also been sent out. The men returned to camp with two deer, which were shared by all. The fresh meat was a welcome change from the dried and canned food diet.

The scent of frying steak wafted over the camp that evening, bringing an unusually intent interest in the supper preparations.

The women had found a berry patch and in short order stripped it clean. The tangy fruit made that special meal seem like a banquet. All were refreshed and ready to begin the journey again.

It took the train three days to reach the Big River. When they finally arrived, Mr. Blake found exactly what he had expected to find—a current far too strong and swift to allow safe wagon passage. He again called a meeting and explained the situation to the entire train. Another camp would have to be made beside the river until the waters subsided. The travelers were all disappointed, but even the most impatient agreed with the decision.

So camp was set up and the people again tried to establish some sort of daily routine to keep boredom from overtaking them. The men formed regular hunting parties and the women again ranged out in search of berries. Missie spent a part of each day gathering wood, as did the women who did not have children to assign to the task. As she gleaned her daily supply, she also added to her stack of surplus piled under her wagon. If the rains should come again, Mrs. Schmidt would not be the only one who was prepared.

Some of the older ladies began to suspect that Missie was "in the family way." Although no comments were made, Missie often noticed the motherly looks that they bestowed upon her. The birth of her baby was almost five months away by Missie's reckoning, and that seemed like a long, long time into the future.

Missie enjoyed the company of Becky Clay. There was no doubt in anyone's mind as to Rebecca's condition, and the women of the train found many little ways to make the girl's work load lighter. Dry sticks were tossed on her pile as the women walked by with their load of wood, extra food was presented at her campfire, and her pail went along to the stream with someone who had a free hand.

Missie felt concern over the travel delay, for Becky's sake. She was hoping with Becky that they would reach Tettsford Junction and the doctor in time. Each day Missie wished that by some miracle the swollen waters would be down and the train could be on its way. But just when the river appeared to be going down, somewhere along its banks another storm would raise the waters again. Day after day passed, and the wagons were still unable to cross. Rafting the wagons to the other side was out of the question in this deep, swift river.

On the fifteenth day by the Big River, the whole camp came alive as another wagon train made its appearance, slowly wending its way down a distant hill. Many went out to meet it. Those who remained behind waited in feverish eagerness for any news that the newcomers might bring.

It was a smaller train than the Blake group and the wagon master seemed a good deal more impatient. After sitting down-river for only two days, he decided that the water had gone down enough for him to get his wagons across. Mr. Blake tried to dissuade him but the man laughed it off, declaring Blake to be as skitterish as an old woman. He had taken wagons across safely when the water had been even higher, he maintained. He then turned to the waiting wagons and ordered the first one over.

Murmured complaints about Mr. Blake were passed through his group of watching drivers—"Here we been a-sittin' when we coulda been days away from here."

The women and children joined the men on the bank to watch the first wagon cross. If it had no trouble crossing, they felt they might all be free to go.

Mr. Blake did not choose to watch. With a look of defeat, and a few well-chosen words directed at the other wagon master, he spun on his heel and marched off.

It seemed for awhile that all would go well with the wagon; and then, to the horror of all of those on the bank, it suddenly hit the deeper water and the current lifted it up and swirled it about. The horses plunged and fought in their effort to swim for the distant shore, but the churning waters were too strong for them. When the driver realized his predicament, he threw himself into the murky deep trying desperately to fight his way to the shore. The wagon, weaving and swaying, was swept downstream as the frantic horses neighed and struggled in their fright. The pitching canvas cover gave one last, sickening heave and then toppled over on its side. The sinking wagon and team were carried downstream and out of sight around a bend in the river.

Meantime, the driver was fighting to keep his head above water. At one point he managed to grab a floating bit of uprooted tree that was also being carried away by the muddy current. A cheer went up from the shore, but the next instant a groan passed through the entire group—the tree struck something under the surface and flipped in midstream, jarring the man loose and leaving him on his own again.

The riverbank became alive with activity as men ran for their horses in an effort to reach near enough to at least throw him a rope. The observers watched the bobbing spot of his dark head as the water swirled him around the river bend. A young woman in the group from the other train collapsed in a heap as the man disappeared, and some of the ladies who travelled with her bent over her to give her assistance.

"Poor woman," Missie gasped. "It must be her man!" She covered her face with her hands and wept.

The body was pulled from the river about a half mile downstream. All attempts to force some life back into the man were futile. The horses and wagon were never seen again.

The following day the travelers from both wagon trains met together; a grave was dug and a service held for the drowned man. His widow had to be helped away from the heaped-up mound that held the body of her young husband. A feeling of helplessness and grief settled over both camps. Respect for Mr. Blake mounted. Eyes were averted when the other wagon master passed by.

A new determination passed through the Blake train: they would wait. They would wait if it took all summer! Horse and wagon were no match for the angry waters.

After breakfast one day a week later, someone in the camp drew their attention to a hill across the river. There on their ponies, faces painted and headdress feathers waving in the wind, sat several Indian braves. The almost-naked bodies glistened in the morning sun. In silence they gazed across the river at the ring of wagons; then, at a signal from their leader, they moved on and out of sight over the hill. Missie shivered as she wondered what could have happened if the swollen river had not been between them. Maybe this was one fulfillment of God's promise, "Yea, I will help thee."

After four weeks of patient and not-so-patient waiting, the

river finally did recede. Mr. Blake, who had carefully watched it each day, crossed it on his horse before he allowed any wagon to put a wheel into the water. When he felt satisfied, the order was given to move out.

It took the whole day to make the crossing. The women and children were taken across on horseback to await the coming of their menfolk and temporary homes. Some of the wagons needed two teams in order to pull them across. Many outriders traveled beside each wagon, steadying it with the many ropes that Mr. Blake insisted upon; thus no wagon got into trouble in midstream from a current that tried to take it sideways rather than forward. Missie couldn't help but remember the tragic death in the other group; if the other wagon master had used such precautions. . . . Mr. Blake was a cautious and experienced wagon master—another of God's provisions.

Once the crossing had been made successfully, the group gathered and Willie offered a prayer of thanks to God for all the travelers. The weary men and animals were glad again to make camp for a good night's rest before taking to the trail. The next day they would resume their journey after their twenty-nine-day delay.

Missie was becoming increasingly concerned about Becky. They still had many days on the trail before reaching Tettsford Junction. Would the services of Mrs. Kosensky be needed after all?

Chapter 11

On the Way Again

Early the next morning, the camp was a bustle of activity. The travelers could hardly wait for the word to move out. Even the horses stamped in their impatience. Missie was surprised at the feelings that clamored within her. During their previous weeks on the trail, she had dreaded the crossing of the Big River, for it seemed to mark the point of no return. But now that it was finally behind them, she was as restless as the teams. She felt like starting out to walk on her own. If she had known the trail and the direction that she was to take, she might have done just that.

Finally the wagons were lined up and the order shouted. The creak of the harnesses and grind of wheels sounded like music to Missie's ears. At last! They were on their way again! All were alive and accounted for. They had crossed the Big River; surely only lesser obstacles lay in their pathway. Since turning back was no longer possible, she was anxious to forge ahead.

Missie could sense Willie's excitement as he carefully guided the team to follow the wagon ahead of him. It was hard for him to restrain himself from urging them on at a faster speed, but no one in the long line of teams was allowed to change the pace set by the wagon master.

The day passed uneventfully. The travelers quickly fell into their familiar routines. But their aching muscles reminded them that they had been idle for too long and must again break in to the rigors of the trail. Missie walked and rode in turn, gathering sticks as she walked; and when she climbed up again to ride, she stashed her bundle under the wagon seat.

At day's end, everyone was weary but tensions were gone. They were moving again and that was what mattered.

As they progressed, the land about them continued its gradual change. There were fewer trees now and those that did grow were smaller than the ones left behind. The women now found very little wood for their fires as they followed the train. They began to carry buckets which they filled with buffalo chips. Missie had preferred the wood which made a much more pleasant fire. Besides, the cumbersome buckets soon had one's arms and back aching.

Occasionally herds of buffalo or deer were seen off in the distance. Twice, Indians were sighted; but though the hearts of the travelers beat more rapidly for a time, these Indians did not approach the train.

The widow of the drowned man, Mrs. Emory, had asked Mr. Blake for permission to join his train. Mr. Blake had found it impossible to refuse her. Arrangements were made for her to share Mr. Weiss' wagon with his daughter Kathy. Mr. Weiss moved in with Henry, and the train moved on.

The unfortunate woman had lost everything in the river—her husband of six months, her home and her belongings. The women of similar size dug into their trunks and showered her with enough garments to outfit her for the remainder of the trip to Tettsford Junction. Though some of the clothes didn't fit very well and weren't particularly fashionable, Mrs. Emory was very grateful for their kindness.

She proved to be a worthy member of the train. Even in her deep sorrow, she was aware of those about her who could use her helping hand. Her quiet manner and helpful acts won her a secure place in the group.

And so they journeyed on. Each day found them a little nearer to their respective destinations, and talk around the fire at night was filled with shared hopes and plans and dreams. The new land held many promises. It seemed to hold out open arms, ready to embrace a stranger—any stranger with hope in his heart and a strong back willing to bend itself to the work.

Chapter 12

Town

Mr. Blake seemed to have a great aversion to towns. In every possible instance he skirted far around them, no matter how small the settlement. When he could not avoid one, he ordered the wagons to keep on moving. No one was allowed to stop for any dallying. Each family made a list of those supplies that were needed and either Mr. Blake or one of his scouts rode into the town and made the purchases.

The wagon master said that his job was to get the wagons, and the folks in them, to Tettsford Junction; and he planned to do just that—and the most deadly enemy of the west-bound settler was a town. Blake had lost no one to swollen rivers, prairie fires or Indians on his many trains west. But he had lost people to *towns*. And since he did not like having his good record smudged, towns were his enemies.

Everyone was surprised, therefore, when Mr. Blake called a meeting of the train members and announced, "Tomorrow we reach Lipton. Ain't much of a town, but we will be stopping there fer a day. Our campsite is to the right of the town within easy walking distance. No teams—no horses atall—no wagons—are to go into the town. Those of you thet have more purchases to make then can be carried will be glad to know thet the Lipton General Store will make deliveries. The place carries a fair line of essentials.

"The train will move on again at the usual hour on Wednesday mornin'. I suggest thet ya all be ready to go."

A general uproar followed the announcement; excitement filled each traveler. To see a town again! To more than just drive through with one's longing eyes picking out dress shops, barbers, food delicacies—just about everything! It would be so good to stop and browse, even though one could spare little money for actual shopping.

Missie's eyes glowed as she and Willie walked back to their wagon. Her mind was busy calculating just what she wanted most and if they would be able to spare their hard-earned cash in order to purchase it.

How big was the town? Did it have a blacksmith? a hairdresser? a butcher? a doctor? Questions flew furiously but Blake was the only one with the answers—and he had somehow disappeared after his announcement.

It was difficult to break from the fires that night and get to bed. Excited chatter buzzed about the camp as women delved into trunks and pulled out favorite dresses. Shaking some of the wrinkles from them, they hung them up in hopes they would be smooth by morning. Men had their wives add another patch to already worn overalls. Some even brushed their shoes, or their hats, or both. Families pored over lists, adding, changing, dreaming, wishing—and reluctantly deleting.

Even the dogs of the camp seemed to catch the fever. They ran back and forth, yapping and tussling and making general nuisances of themselves.

The next morning everyone was ready to roll long before the call was given—even the often tardy Standards. The sooner they began the journey, the sooner Lipton would be reached—and the longer the time available for shopping.

The wagons lumbered out, set for another long, hot, dusty day on the trail, everyone hoping that it wouldn't be too late when they pulled into camp to be off to the town.

To everyone's amazement and delight, the town lay before them as they topped the first hill. They had camped only a few miles from it the night before! They all laughed at themselves and at their wagon master, but Mr. Blake's face remained as impassive as ever.

They soon reached the new campsite and formed their customary circle. The men set about the task of caring for the animals while the women scurried around, building fires to heat water for sponge baths within the confines of their wagons. By the time they and their children were ready to head into town, the sun had climbed high into the clear sky; it would be another extremely warm day.

They departed in little groups, eager and expectant. Henry accompained some of the younger people. The Collinses walked together, Sissie with Meggie in her arms and Tom with Joey hoisted on his shoulders. Mrs. Thorne strode off, with her offspring matching her long strides; her husband would have none of the foolishness and elected to stay behind and mend the harness. Mrs. Page, after voicing a parting barb at Jessie Tuttle, hurried down the trail without even waiting for a reply. Tillie Crane went along, too impatient to wait even for her young husband—at last she could have *something* done to her hair! Mrs. Schmidt threw a bundle of hastily gathered sticks under the protection of her wagon, shook out her apron and started off with her family members: they quickly overtook and passed the slowmoving Mrs. Kosensky.

Missie and Willie walked with John and Becky. They chose a much slower pace for Becky's sake, though they too were impatient.

As they passed the Weiss' wagon, they saw Mrs. Emory fastening the tent flap down before leaving for town. Her sad face was lit by a smile when she saw the young couples. Without a word, Willie stepped over to lend her a hand.

"Eager to git into town?" She directed her question to the women.

"Oh, yes," Becky bubbled. "It seems like forever since I've walked on a board sidewalk or looked in a shop."

Mrs. Emory just smiled.

She is so attractive when she smiles like that, thought Missie, *and so very young. I reckon she's not much older than I am. What would I do if something happened to my Willie? How would I ever get home again? Would I just be stranded somewhere out here in the West?* Just the thought of such a thing made Missie's stomach churn. *Dear God,* she prayed inwardly, *I don't think I could stand it.*

Then she thought of her own mother. A new awareness of what Marty had been through those long years before filled her being and tears threatened to fill her eyes. She hurriedly blinked them away before anyone could notice them.

"Are you goin' shoppin', too?" she asked Mrs. Emory.

The woman's face sobered some and she shook her head.

"Not exactly," she replied.

Missie realized that the woman would probably have nothing to go shopping with, even though her needs were great.

There was silence for a minute. The young woman seemed to be deciding if she should speak, or leave her thoughts unsaid.

Finally she spoke, her voice soft and even, "I—I'm really goin' to look for a church. I—have this need for a place of prayer."

It was Willie who then reached for the woman's hand. He said nothing—just looked deeply into her eyes and gently squeezed the small hand in both of his calloused, manly ones. Missie blinked back more tears. The woman withdrew her hand; with a slight nod of her head that sent the glistening tears on her lashes spilling down her cheeks, she turned to go.

Missie reached for Willie's hand then. He was so much like her pa, her Willie. He felt so deeply what others were feeling. Homesickness for her father and a surge of love for Willie swept through Missie in one wave.

They turned to follow the Clays who were already walking slowly down the path toward town.

"Willie," Missie whispered, "we should try an' draw her out more. She's such a sweet thing, the poor soul. I can't imagine anyone sufferin' so much—so young."

"Yer ma an' pa did," Willie reminded her gently. His hand tightened on hers.

Missie was silent, too deeply moved to try to speak. Yes, her ma and pa had suffered, but she had been too young to be aware of it. She only remembered them as laughing, loving parents. Would Mrs. Emory someday be able to laugh and love again, too? Missie prayed that the town could supply her with a fine little church where she could meet with God.

The town wasn't much, as towns go, but to the travelers it would suffice. There were sidewalks for Becky to walk on, although one needed to watch one's step—there were loose and broken, even missing, boards. The shoppers soon learned to keep an eye on where they next intended to step.

After a quick general look at the town, the couples separated. The ladies went to yearn over threads, yarn, yard goods and other "luxuries." The men went off to the livery stable to check on more "practical" supplies.

Becky and Missie spent a long part of their morning surveying the soft yarns and materials, planning and dreaming of what they would make for their coming babies. Becky already had most of her necessities, her baby having been "expected" before she ever left home, but she was eager to add some special things to the baby's wardrobe. Missie would wait for her main preparation until she reached Willie's land and was settled—but it would be so much fun to work on a few things now.

There was a hotel of sorts in Lipton, and Becky and Missie's menfolk had promised to take their wives there for a meal. They all looked forward to it eagerly. It would be so good to have food that didn't taste of wood smoke, real store-bought tea, meat that wasn't wild, and maybe even some fresh bread. And vegetables! How long it had been since they had tasted fresh vegetables!

Promptly at noon the men returned and made an elaborate display of escorting their women to the dining room. The room was already crowded, and they had to wait for a table.

The four deliberated long over the menu, and finally, at the impatience of the waitress, placed their orders. Missie was surprised at how flat things tasted without the tang of the smoke. The bread was not fresh—but it *was* bread. The meat was mild enough—but more than a little tough, and the vegetables were definitely overcooked. However, they enjoyed it immensely, and pretended to one another that it was the finest they had ever eaten. They even ordered pie and lingered over it, savoring each bite as they slowly sipped their cups of tea.

In the afternoon they inspected the stores again. They knew that wise decisions had to be made and that each purchase must be considered carefully. It was a big job to make up one's mind after not having shopped for so long.

Their lists were consulted, changed and finally the goods were ordered. Necessary foods were restocked and a few fresh vegetables were purchased. Missie did pick out a few soft flannels and cottons for her sewing for the coming baby and also bought additional wool for heavy socks. They began their walk back, weary and a little poorer, but refreshed by their day spent back in the "real world." They clutched in their arms a few of their most cherished purchases. They would eagerly wait for the rest to be delivered that evening.

Missie and Willie left John and Becky at their wagon and walked on to their own. Becky was looking tired after her exciting and busy day—this in spite of the fact that Missie had insisted she sit and rest for a spell every so often throughout the time spent in town. Missie called back and invited them to share the evening meal with them so that Becky might get some much needed rest. Becky was happy to accept.

Upon reaching the wagon, Missie stowed away her purchases and set to work building the fire and preparing the meal. Willie changed back into his old overalls and went to care for the cows and horses.

It had been a good day. Missie hummed as she worked. She could hear Willie's whistle moving down the path toward the draw where the animals were staked out to graze.

Chapter 13

Breaking Camp

The usual order of the camp was not in evidence the next morning. The 'town,' as Mr. Blake feared, had produced its casualties. Tillie Crane had found her hairdresser. She had also found a job in a dress shop, and she adamantly refused to move one more step into that "God-forsaken" land of wind, sun and rain. Her husband had spent the night badgering and pleading by turn, but nothing was to make Tillie change her mind. A broken Jason Crane finally came to inform Mr. Blake that their wagon would be withdrawing. There was no way that he would travel on without his wife. He'd see what he could do for a job in Lipton. Surely there was work somewhere for a man who was willing.

The Cranes weren't the only ones with problems. A number of the men from the train had been "out on the town." Most of them staggered in, sometime during the night, in various stages of disrepair. Mrs. Kosensky had taken care of her husband—a cold bucket of water for his outside, several cups of hot coffee for his inside. The next morning he was bleary-eyed and belligerent, but ready for travel.

Jessie Tuttle handled her driver-brother, J.M. Dooley, simply by stuffing him into the wagon and hitching the team herself.

Mrs. Thorne had the most trouble. Her husband failed to reappear at all. After waiting tight-lipped, she set off for town in search of her errant man but strode back to camp empty-handed after two hours of searching. It was Mr. Blake's turn. Maybe he was more familiar with where to look; at any rate, after about three quarters of an hour, he returned. The livery wagon followed, delivering a very sodden Mr. Thorne. His wife said nothing, simply nodding to the men where Mr. Thorne was to be placed and picking up the reins of her team.

After three hours of delay, the teams finally moved out. By then the sun was already hot, the children cranky, and the adults out-of-sorts.

Mrs. Thorne did not so much as give her neighbors a nod or a suggestion of apology. She smacked her team smartly with a rein and maneuvered into position, her face stern and her eyes straight ahead.

Missie shook her head as the woman drove by her. It had been told that Mrs. Thorne had known all along her husband wouldn't remain in the camp mending harness and that she knew exactly what he would do once he got to town. It had happened many times in the past and would likely happen often in the future.

Missie was sure that the invincible Mrs. Thorne would be able to cope. Nothing seemed to shake that woman from solid-rock indifference.

Mrs. Thorne smacked her team again and passed on by, her hands steady, her eyes unblinking against the glare of the mid-morning sun. Missie almost missed it, but it was there—and what she saw made her stop short and catch her breath; for unmistakably running down the coarse, tanned cheeks of the woman was a steady stream of tears.

When Missie could breathe again she whispered, "Ya poor soul. Here ya are a hurtin' an' nobody knows—nobody even suspects, so no one reaches out to you in understandin'. Oh . . . God forgive me. Forgive me for not seein' past her stiff jaw to the hurts and the needs. Help me to help her, Lord—to show her kindness and love. She needs me. She needs *You*, Lord."

Thereafter, Missie took every opportunity that she could find to greet the woman with a smile, to show little acts of kindness in any way that she could.

The older woman did not really melt, but she did begin to show a little softness around the firm, hard edges of her soul.

Chapter 14

Rebecca

They had been on the trail four days since leaving Lipton, and seemed to be making good progress. The men who had visited the tavern had sobered up, and were now back to their hard tasks. But it was strongly suspected that J.M. Dooley had somehow managed to smuggle some whiskey along in his wagon—against Mr. Blake's orders. It was a real source of contention between J.M. and Jessie Tuttle; and, of course, anything that affected Jessie, Mrs. Page considered her right to become involved in as well. So, a three-way war was now raging.

Folks smiled at the ridiculousness of it all, but finally Mr. Blake decided that it was time to step in. J.M.'s booze was discovered and discarded. Mrs. Page and her wagon were assigned a new position at the end of the line far from Jessie Tuttle. Things seemed to settle down again.

When they made camp the fourth night, a message was sent to Missie as she cleaned up after the evening meal. It was carried by Mrs. Kosensky's daughter, Nell.

"Ma says, could ya come to Mrs. Clay? She been in labor

most of the afternoon, an' wants to see ya."

Missie's eyes opened wide in surprise. She had missed Becky that day but had supposed that she just didn't feel up to taking in her customary short walk. She called over to Henry to tell Willie where she would be and quickly reached inside the wagon for a shawl. She almost ran in her eagerness to get to Becky, but held herself back lest others watching would be unduly concerned by her haste.

As she approached the wagon, she could hear Becky's soft crying. She ran the last few steps and was met by a very worried-looking Mrs. Kosensky. Instead of inviting Missie up, the other woman climbed down. She drew Missie aside and began to speak in a whisper.

"Ain't good, Ma'am, ain't good. Me—I deliver babies. Yes, lotsa babies—but this kind, no. He small—he twisted—and he early." She shook her head, and Missie noticed tears in her eyes. "Ain't good. She need a doctor—bad."

"May I see her?" Missie begged, longing to be a source of comfort and aid to Becky.

"Yes—yes, do."

Missie brushed by the woman, and scrambled up into the wagon. Becky was flushed and damp with perspiration. Missie looked at her pale face in alarm. She reached for Becky's hand, and then began to smooth back her long, loose hair. She spoke softly. She really wasn't aware of what she said to Becky, but it seemed to comfort the anguished girl.

Missie stayed with Becky for most of the night, but the situation did not improve. Occasionally, Becky seemed to drift off into a troubled sleep but she was soon reawakened by her discomfort. At length, Willie, who had come to wait outside by the fire with John, suggested that Missie should get some rest or she would be in danger, too. Mrs. Kosensky agreed.

The next morning the LaHayes crawled wearily from their bed and began the preparations for another day on the trail. Missie sent Willie over to ask about Becky. He returned with the news that nothing had changed. Missie's heart felt heavy as she continued preparing their breakfast.

While she was hurrying to pack up their belongings, one of the trail scouts came by on his horse. He stopped at each wagon with the same message.

"Mr. Blake says we stay put today. He's not breakin' camp 'til thet baby's arrived."

Missie felt much relief and would have willingly hugged the grisly wagon master. She could not imagine what it would be like for Becky if she had to bounce around in a moving wagon.

The day dragged on. A rider had been sent back to Lipton the night before to see if a doctor could be found and brought to the camp. Everyone who knew how, and even some who didn't, prayed that there might be a doctor and that he would arrive soon.

The women tried to keep busy with a little wagon cleaning and men checked harnesses and wheels. Neighbors used the long hours as an excuse to sit and discuss anything that came to mind. Still the time only crawled; by the time the day was coming to an end, everyone's nerves were on edge. Becky and her unborn baby were a heavy concern on everyone's mind.

With no more valid reason to stay up, they finally extinguished their campfires and went to bed, hoping that the good news of the baby's birth would reach them during the night.

It did not happen.

As they stirred about the camp the next morning, the news spread quickly that the child had not yet been born. Another long day began. With no harnesses to mend and no further wagon cleaning to be done, time lay heavy on hands and minds. Yet hope remained alive. Surely with more delay the doctor from Lipton would have plenty of time to make it. But the rider finally returned, tired and dusty and with a weary, limping horse. There was no doctor in Lipton.

It was almost one-thirty in the afternoon when Mrs. Kosensky climbed down from the Clay wagon. Willie, Missie and several other neighbors had been waiting outside. No one had heard the cry of a newborn baby. Mrs. Kosensky's shoulders sagged and tears coursed down her plump cheeks. To the waiting friends she shook her head.

"No," she said brokenly. "No—he did not make it, the little one."

"Oh, Becky!" cried Missie, "poor Becky. She'll be heart-broken."

"No," said Mrs. Kosensky, again shaking her head. "No. The little mama—she did not make it either."

For a moment Missie chose not to understand, not to believe. But she knew, as she looked at the older woman, that the news was indeed true. Then, from the depths of the covered wagon, came the muffled sobs of a man.

"Oh, dear God," Missie prayed, putting her hands to her face and letting the tears flow freely. Then she turned to bury her face against Willie's shoulder, and he held her close for a time and let her weep. When her spasm of tears seemed spent, he gently put her from him.

"I must go in to John," he said. "Can you make it to the wag-on alone?"

Missie nodded, but it was Henry who led her away, easing her over the rough terrain and opening the canvas flap so that she could step into the wagon.

She laid herself down in the stuffy heat and let the tears wash away the sorrow and confusion in her soul.

The funeral service was held the next morning. John stood in stunned silence as the young mother and her infant son were laid together in a blanket. Shock and grief had numbed his mind, and he didn't seem to comprehend the event.

After the service was over, the wagons were quietly ordered to move out. The men guided their animals into line silently, thoughtfully. Willie had suggested that John ride with them for a while but he preferred to be alone. Missie rode beside Willie, but they had not gone far before she asked to be let down.

She stood quietly for a time, letting the wagons roll past her, turning her back to the dust swirling from their wheels. When the last one had gone by, Missie looked back the way that they had come. In the valley below was the circle where they had camped. The evidence of a recent train was still there—the trampled grass, the campfire ashes, the wheel marks—and there, just to the left, was the little mound of bare earth marking the spot where they had left Becky. For a moment Missie wanted to run back; but she knew that it was pointless. Becky was gone from them now. Missie felt some measure of comfort in the thought that Becky was not alone. Beneath the earth, she held in her arms her baby boy.

"Good-bye, Becky," Missie whispered. "Good-bye, Rebecca Clay. You were a dear, sweet friend. May you—and your little one—find great pleasure and comfort in the house of God." And with tears streaming down her cheeks, Missie turned to follow the wagons.

Just as Missie turned to go, a lone rider emerged from the bushes in the valley and stopped beside the soft mound. Missie recognized the form of Mr. Blake. The man dismounted from his horse and approached the new grave. He removed his hat and stood momentarily with bowed head. Then he bent down and placed a small cluster of prairie flowers on the fresh earth. As he turned and mounted his horse, Missie felt a fresh stream of tears slide down her cheeks.

That was a lovely thing to do, she thought.

But Missie had no way of knowing that many years ago, the same man had stood beside another mound—one that held his own wife and infant son. At that time, too, he had been forced to ride away and leave them to lie alone beside a prairie trail.

Chapter 15

A Tough Decision

There was a measure of comfort in the fact that Tettsford Junction was getting nearer and nearer, but the days always seemed long. Missie kept herself occupied as much as she could. She carefully looked after her own responsibilities, as well as devoting much time to helping others—especially Mrs. Collins. The two youngsters kept quite healthy, in spite of the rigors of the trail; but they still required a lot of time and attention.

Missie and Willie had not yet been able to talk about Becky. Missie cried often. If Willie was there when she cried, he held her close, stroking her hair and listening with his heart. They both realized that sometime—and sometime soon—they must discuss it. Hopefully, their hearts could then begin to heal.

John Clay was always included in Willie's evening prayer. But though Missie ached for John, she also realized that she felt a twinge of resentment toward him.

One night, after they had retired, Willie gently broached the subject.

"It easin' some 'bout Becky?"

His arm tightened around Missie as he asked the question. He wanted her to know that he understood, and that he suffered with her.

"I guess—some," Missie was able to answer without a flood of tears.

"I think maybe it's gittin' harder for John," Willie continued after a few moments of silence.

"How?"

"Well, at first I don't think it was real to John. Now it is. He's over the shock-like; an' he's missin' Becky—knowin' thet she won't be back, won't be his—ever again."

Missie pondered Willie's words. That small feeling of anger toward John stirred within her. She decided to express it.

"John was too sure of himself, too cocky 'bout Becky an' that baby. Just 'cause his mother . . . Things can go wrong—they can. He should have known that." Missie couldn't hold back her tears.

"I was feelin' those same thoughts," Willie said gently, "but maybe we're too hard on John. Sure he was cocky. But, maybe it was just cover-up, to sorta make things happen the way he wanted them to. I don't know. All I know is thet he loved Becky—very much—an' he wanted thet son—very much. An' now he has neither of them—an' he's truly sorrowin', Missie. Maybe we're all guilty of holdin' too lightly those thet we love."

Missie's sobs quieted as she thought on Willie's words. He was right, of course. John did love Becky and he had wanted the baby. It was no fault of John's that things had gone wrong. If it hadn't been for the long delay at the Big River, they would have reached Tettsford Junction and the doctor on time—even with Becky's baby coming early.

A feeling of great sorrow for John swept over Missie. The poor man—to lose so much. She must pray for him more.

Willie interrupted her thoughts.

"Missie—"

When he didn't continue, she turned toward him; but it was too dark in the wagon to read his face.

"I been thinkin'," he finally continued. "When we git to Tettsford Junction, there's a doc there."

"I know."

"I want ya to have a doc, Missie."

"But our baby is almost four months away," Missie purposely exaggerated just a bit.

"I know."

Missie thought on it. "Reckon we could," she finally stated. "How far is yer land from Tettsford Junction?"

"Good week's travel by wagon."

"A week? Reckon I could stand that."

"That's not what I had in mind, Missie," Willie said slowly.

"What *did* you have in mind?"

Willie swallowed. "Well, I figured thet maybe ya should stay at Tettsford until after the baby is safely delivered."

"But you're in a great hurry to get to the land—to put up some corrals, fix a house, and get yourself some cattle before winter. . . ."

"Ya, Missie, but—"

"That'd make you late and rushed. By the time I'm ready to travel and we make the trip, you'd hardly have time—"

Willie interrupted. "I'd go on as planned, Missie, an' see to all those things."

"An' leave me behind?" Missie could scarcely believe her ears.

"It's the only way, Missie—far as I can see."

"But I don't want—"

Willie's arm tightened again, but his voice was firm. "I don't want it either, Missie, but it's the only way. I'm not takin' any chances like John took. I—"

But Missie quickly stopped him. "It's not the same—can't you see? Becky was sick-like from the beginnin'. Me—I've been fine all along."

Missie felt Willie's hand grip her shoulder.

"It *could happen* thet ya need a doctor. There are no doctors where we're goin'. There aren't even neighbors who could be midwives. There's no one to help ya, Missie. No one! Can't ya see? I can't take ya there. Not after what's happened!"

A sob caught in Missie's throat but she tried one more time.

"Then we'll just have to go back to Tettsford when the time

comes. I don't want to stay without you, Willie. We'll just have to go back."

"An' iffen the baby comes early—like Becky's? How will we know when it's time? Something could go wrong *any time*. Already, I pray every night thet you'll be fine fer the next day's travel, fine 'til we reach Tettsford. Iffen I take ya on from there, down to the ranch with the idea of bringin' ya back—What iffen we're caught on the trail? What then?"

Missie knew that she had lost, for the moment. She didn't bother to argue anymore, but buried her face against Willie's shoulder and wept. To be without Willie for three long months or more, in a strange town, waiting all alone—how could she ever bear it?

She felt a tear drop gently onto her forehead. Willie was weeping too.

"It's gonna be so hard," he finally said huskily. "So awful hard—but we'll make it. Remember our verse—'Fear thou not; for I am with thee: be not dismayed; for I am thy God: I will strengthen thee; yea, I will help thee; yea, I will uphold thee with the right hand of my righteousness!' "

Chapter 16

Tettsford Junction

The wagon train made its final camp just outside of Tettsford Junction. The town proved to be a larger settlement than anyone on the train had anticipated. Missie wondered what sustained it after she noted the bleakness of the countryside. The land about didn't appear able to produce any more than a bit of sagebrush. *Who could possibly endure such barrenness?* Missie thought. She turned her back to the wind that seemed to be constantly blowing.

The traveling companions of many weeks shared mixed emotions. John still felt empty and alone. He had difficulty deciding what he should do, whether to continue on his way and join his brother, or look for some kind of work in the town. The promises that the land held seemed empty now that Becky was gone.

The Pages made up their minds to stay in town, as did a couple of other families that Missie didn't know very well. Jessie Tuttle would continue on, so Mrs. Page saved a few choice words to hurl as a parting shot. Jessie ignored the needling, much to Mrs. Page's annoyance.

Mrs. Emory, the young widow, knew that she had very few options open to her. She would stay in the town. The kindness of the members of the wagon train had gotton her to Tettsford Junction; now it was up to her to take care for herself. She had blossomed and matured during her days on the trail and though she still felt the loss of her husband, she seemed prepared to face life again.

Mr. Weiss and Kathy also decided to remain in Tettsford. Mr. Weiss declared with certainty that such a busy town would be able to use another smithy. Missie wondered if that was the real reason—or if he had developed a secret attachment to the young widow and was willing to bide his time. She rather hoped not. Melinda Emory was scarcely older than Mr. Weiss' daughter, Kathy. However, it was their business, Missie decided, and Mr. Weiss was a very kind man.

Most of the other travelers would be leaving in a few days' time with other trains, traveling northwest to the "prairies." Missie couldn't see how any place could be more *prairie* than where they were at present, and how anyone could actually *choose* to live here. But she did not voice her feelings.

Willie asked Missie if she wanted to go in and see the town, as soon as camp was made and the neccessary tasks performed. But she was remembering her last visit to town in the company of Becky, and was thinking ahead to her own dreaded stay in this one.

She declined, and went to her wagon to be alone.

If only Willie would change his mind! Did he expect her to spend three or more miserable months cooped up in this horrible wagon? In this dreary town, with the sun beating relentlessly on the shadeless landscape and the wind howling constantly about the canvas flaps? If only she had known ahead of time that Willie wouldn't be taking her on to his land, to help build a home and establish his ranch. She might as well have stayed at home with her own folks who loved her and would have provided for her. *Why trek halfway 'cross the world and suffer all of the heat, the rain, the mosquitoes, the blistered and aching feet—just to be dumped off here?* Her thoughts tumbled round and round in her mind. It just wasn't fair of Willie. It wasn't fair at all.

Missie let the hot tears course down her face and finally fell
into an exhausted sleep.

When Willie returned, he was elated and started calling to
her even before he had entered the wagon. "I've found a place!"
he almost whooped. Missie jerked to attention.

"A place for *what*?"

"For you," he declared, surprised at her question. "For you—
while yer waitin'."

She stared at him. So Willie hadn't ever planned for her to
spend these months ahead in the wagon.

Missie didn't tell him that she still didn't intend to *wait*.
She intended to *go*. But deep inside she knew that it was useless
to fight it.

"It's only one room—but it's a nice, fair size. An' it's with fine
folks. I'm sure thet you'll like 'em, an' they even said that I can
stay there, too, 'til the supply train is ready to leave."

"That's right good of 'em," Missie said with spark, "seein'
how you *are* my husband."

Willie ignored the remark and hurried on. "Mr. Taylorson
runs a general store an' his wife teaches a bit of piano. Says ya
might even learn to play the piano while yer a-waitin'."

"Oh, Willie!" Missie said in exasperation. "What in heaven's
name would I want to learn piano for? What good would that do
me where—"

"It would help fill in the long hours," Willie interposed. "It
might help a heap, iffen ya choose to let it." His words were mild
but he gave her a searching look.

Missie wanted to flounce off, but there was no place to go—
neighbors' eyes were watching all around. So she turned her back
on Willie and began to trim the wick of the lantern which usually
sat on the outside shelf, making sure that she looked at ease and
composed.

Willie continued, "The doc lives only three houses down from
the Taylorsons, so he'll be right handy when—"

"Iffen he's not off somewhere settin' a broken leg or treatin' a
bullet wound," Missie retorted.

"Guess thet could happen even back home," Willie said
calmly. "But there are two midwives in town—'case he should be
away. I inquired."

"Midwife didn't help Becky none."

Missie grimaced at her shrewishness. She was being unfair to Willie. She knew that. He was doing what he believed was right. She blinked back her tears and steadied her voice.

"An' when does the supply train go?" She deliberately changed the course of the conversation.

" 'Bout a week—maybe a little less."

"An' you'll be ready?"

"Plan to be. Think I'll do like yer pa suggested. I'll pick me up another wagon with the rails fer the corrals an' other supplies. That way, I won't be held up none once I git to our land."

"An' where would this treeless town ever get rails for a corral?" Missie couldn't keep her dislike for the place from her voice.

"They haul 'em in. Lots of folks need 'em. Guess there's lumber a lot closer than it looks—some of those hills to the west are treed."

Missie nodded.

"Well, I'd best see to the stock," Willie said and turned to go, then turned back again. "Henry said to let ya know he won't be here fer supper."

"What's he plannin'?"

"He's eatin' with the Weisses. But what he's *plannin'*—who knows?"

Missie smiled in spite of herself. So it was Kathy Weiss that Henry had taken a shine to. He had kept her guessing the whole trip, seeming to give equal attention to more than one girl. Well, at least Kathy also would be staying on in Tettsford—Missie would be assured of some company.

As she began work on the evening meal, she regretted her refusal to go into town. She could have been cooking something special and fresh for supper, instead of the same old fare—if she hadn't chosen to remain at the wagon feeling mistreated and sorry for herself.

She was bored with the food; she was bored with the wagon; she was even bored with her neighbors. Tomorrow she *would* go into town. She might even let Willie introduce her to the Taylorsons. It wasn't their fault that she would be stuck here in the town until the baby arrived. Not their fault at all.

Chapter 17

The Taylorsons

Missie awoke refreshed the next morning. She determined to make the best of the day. She washed carefully and chose one of her favorite dresses for her venture into town. Loose and full, with a sash that tied in the back, the small print was cheerful and becoming. Missie felt relieved that it would be usable throughout her confinement—though it wouldn't be as stylish as when it showed off her slim waist. The loose shirtwaists and expandable skirts that Missie and her mama had prepared for "some future day" when Missie would be needing them were all right for everyday wear. But Missie was not too taken with the plain, simple dark skirts and was thankful that she had a nice assortment of aprons to wear over them. She combed her hair with particular care and began to prepare breakfast for the men.

Henry was the first to appear. He seemed to approve of how Missie looked.

"See yer not wearin' yer hikin' shoes today," he teased.

Missie looked down at her trim feet carefully encased in smart black boots. She smiled.

"I just may *never* wear 'em again," she answered.

"Now, now," Henry replied, "ya sure wouldn't want thet part of yer edjication to jest go to waste, would ya?"

"Seems every *other* part of my education has gone to waste," Missie responded. There was a quiver in her voice as she thought of her classroom of eager children back home.

"Not so," Henry was quick to say. "Don't fergit thet you'll soon be 'teacher' agin."

Missie glanced down at her blossoming figure and flushed. Henry quickly changed the subject.

"See'd the town yet?"

"Not yet—but Willie has. I didn't feel much like goin' in yesterday. I'm more ready-like today."

Henry nodded.

"Big place really—but not too fancy."

"Where'd they get the name?"

"Man named Tettsford first set up a store there to catch the trade of the wagons goin' through."

"He still there?"

"Naw. He made his money, then cleared out. Went back East—to spend it, I guess."

"Smart man," Missie said under her breath.

"Ya know what I'm gonna miss most 'bout wagon-trainin'?"

Henry's abrupt change of subject surprised Missie; but she soon recovered and answered with a teasing voice, "Now, *I* wonder."

Henry blushed.

"Naw," he said, "nothin' like thet. I'm gonna miss the Sunday gatherin's."

Missie sobered.

"I guess I will, too," she said. "They weren't nothin' like home, but they were special in their own way, weren't they? An' you did a first-rate job, Henry. A real good job. Did you ever think of bein' a preacher?"

Henry's blush deepened. "I thought on it—sorta. But I ain't got what it takes to be a preacher. Very little book learnin' and not much civilizin' either."

"That's not true, Henry! You're a born leader. Didn't you

notice how the people followed you, accepted you, expected you to take the lead?"

Henry sat silently. "They did, some," he agreed. "But thet was a wagon train, not a settlement church. There's a heap of difference there. I did decide one thing, though . . ." He hesitated.

"Bein'?" Missie prompted.

"Well, I jest told the Lord thet iffen He had a place fer me—wherever it was—I'd be happy to do whatever I could. I don't expect it to be in a church, Missie—but there's lots of folks who need God who never come a-lookin' fer Him in a church."

"I'm glad, Henry," Missie said softly. "I'm glad you feel that way. And you're right; God needs lots of us—everywhere—to touch other people's hearts."

Missie turned back to tend the breakfast and Henry settled himself on a low stool. It wasn't long until Missie heard a cheery whistle and knew that Willie would soon join them.

Willie's eyes brightened when he saw Missie. His whistle changed abruptly. Then he grinned.

"Yer lookin' right smart this mornin', Mrs LaHaye."

"Oh, Willie, stop teasin'. You've been seein' me in plain dresses an' walkin' shoes for so long that you've forgotten what I really look like."

"Then I hope ya remind me often. Looks good, don't she, Henry?" Willie said with a wink.

"I already told her so."

"Oh, ho," Willie laughed. "Now thet the young Miss Weiss has favored yer presence, ya think thet ya can pass out compliments to all of the womenfolk, do ya?"

"Nope," said Henry. "Jest the *special* ones."

Willie laughed again. "Well, she's special, all right."

He kissed Missie on the cheek. Missie leaned primly away. "Really, Willie," she reprimanded. "We don't need to put on a show for all to see." She busied herself with serving the breakfast.

After they had eaten, and read a portion of scripture—which Willie ended as he had throughout the journey with the special passage given to them by Missie's father—and had prayer together, Missie began clearing up.

"Will ya be needin' me today?" Henry asked Willie.

Willie thought a moment.

"No, I can manage carin' fer the stock. Go ahead. Make any plans thet ya care to."

"Thanks. I reckon I'll give the Weisses a hand at gettin' settled in town. They did manage to find a house—such as it is."

"Is Mrs. Emory gonna stay with 'em?"

"No, and she needs some settlin' too. She found a small room over the general store, but there's not much furniture there to speak of. She's already signed up to teach school come fall; but, until then, she's gonna work in the hotel kitchen."

"The kitchen? Seems rather heavy, burdensome work for such a genteel little woman," Missie commented doubtfully.

"Thet's what I thought. But the job is there—an she insists."

Missie detected genuine concern in Henry's voice. He put on his hat.

"Well, iffen yer sure I'm not needed, I'll git on over there an' give 'em a hand."

"He's got it right bad, hasn't he?" Willie remarked after Henry had walked away. "Well, Mrs. LaHaye, may I escort ya into town? I take it ya didn't git all prettied up jest to sit out in the sun."

"I think, sir, that I might consent to that," Missie replied archly.

Missie found the town much as she had expected. There seemed to be very little that was green. A few small gardens looked up thirstily at the sun-drenched sky. The vegetables that fought for an existence were dwarfed and scraggly. Here and there some brave grass put in an appearance—under a dripping pump or close to a watering trough. As far as Missie could see, there had been no attempt to plant trees or shrubbery. Puffs of dust scattered whenever the wind stirred.

The buildings, too, were bleak. No bright paint or fancy signs. Square, bold letters spelled SALOON over a gray, wind-worn wood building. Another plain sign read HOTEL. Missie winced to think of Melinda Emory working there in a hot, stuffy kitchen. Several other weathered buildings lined the dusty streets. There were sidewalks, fairly new-looking, but they too were layered with dust where the women's skirts had not whisked them clean.

There was more than one saloon. In fact, as Missie let her eyes search down the street, she counted five. *What does such a town need with five saloons?* she wondered. It certainly was not as blessed with churches, but Missie did spy a small spire reaching up from among the buildings huddled over to her left.

There were blacksmith shops—at least three—but maybe, as Mr. Weiss had said, a town this size could use another.

There was also a bank, a sheriff's office, a printshop, a telegraph office, liveries, a stagecoach landing, and an assortment of stores and other buildings that Missie had not yet identified. Missie smiled as she read the notice, "Overland Stagecoaches," and wondered where on earth they could take a body.

The town didn't interest her much at this point. She still dreaded the fact that she had to stay in it for three months, or more, without Willie. She didn't want this town. She wanted Willie's land, the place where she intended to make a home. It would be so different there. The cool valley, the green grass and Willie's beloved hills, rolling away to the mountains. Missie could hardly wait for a look at those mountains.

"The Taylorsons live jest down here," Willie announced, disturbing her thoughts. He made a right-hand turn. Soon they were walking down a street lined with houses. There were no sidewalks, but the street was smooth, though dusty.

"Thet there is where the doc lives. He has a couple a' rooms for his office in the sheriff's, but he also has one room there at the front of his house fer off-hour treatin'."

Missie let her glance slide over the doctor's residence. The house was unpretentious.

"An' here we are," Willie said, and opened a gate. Missie stared at the house. It was of unpainted lumber, big and sturdy-looking, but as barren as the rest of the town. They passed by a bit of a garden that seemed to be struggling valiantly for existence. Missie's thoughts returned to Marty's full, healthy, vegetable garden at home.

"My, things be dry!" she ventured.

"They git a little short on water here 'bouts."

Willie rapped on the door and a plump, pleasant-faced woman answered.

"Oh," she said with a smile, "ya brought yer little wife." Her gaze traveled over Missie. "She do be in the family way, all right."

Missie felt the color rush to her face.

"This be Mrs. Taylorson, Missie," Willie said, attempting to ease over the situation. "An' this be my wife—Mrs. LaHaye."

Missie was glad that Willie had introduced her as *Mrs. LaHaye.* Somehow it made her feel more grown-up and less like an awkward schoolgirl.

"Come on in," Mrs. Taylorson said, "an' I'll show ya yer room."

She turned and clumped up the stairs that were to the left of the hall, puffing as she climbed. At the top of the stairs she again took a left turn and pushed open a door. The room was stifling hot; not a bit of air stirred the curtains. It was a plain room, but it was clean. The bed looked old, but rather comfortable. Mrs. Taylorson was a no-nonsense person.

"Yer husband said thet ya had yer own things," said Mrs. Taylorson, "so I jest took out the beddin', an' such."

"Yes, I do," Missie answered, wondering why the faded curtains at the window had escaped Mrs. Taylorson's clean sweep. "It will be just fine."

"I don't usually keep boarders," she said, "but yer husband seemed in a real need-like. An' he said thet ya were clean—an' sensible. So I says, 'Okay, I'll give it a try.'

"One must have rules, though, when one has boarders, so I've made 'em up an' posted 'em here. Don't expect this third one will bother ya much, ya bein' the way ya are, but one never knows— an' one needs rules. I'll leave ya now to look over things an' decide what ya want to be a bringin' in. I'll go put on some tea."

She stepped out of the room and they were alone.

Missie wanted to cry but she fought it. She must keep herself well in hand.

Willie hurried over to the window and threw it wide open. Missie turned to the posted list.

"Oh, oh," she said, "you just broke rule number one."

Willie was at her side.

"Number one," Missie read, " 'Do not leave window open; the dust blows in!'

"Number two, 'No loud talking or laughing.'"

"Number three, 'No having men to your room or going out with them, 'cepting your husband.'"

"Number four, 'All water must be used *at least twice* before it is thrown out. We're powerful short, you know.'"

"Number five, 'Mealtimes are 8:00, 12:30 and 6:00, and must be strictly kept. It bothers Mr. T's ulcer iffen he is kept waiting.'"

"Number six, 'Bedtime is 10:00.'"

"Number seven, 'Borders'—look at the spellin' of that; makes me feel like a bunch of petunias.—'Borders are expected to attend church on Sundays.'"

"Number eight, 'Rent must be paid in advance.'"

"Number nine, 'No borrowing money or property.'"

"Number ten, 'Border must care for her own personal needs and clothes.'"

"Number eleven, 'Hair can be washed at back door basin— once a week.'"

"Number twelve—I guess she ran out of ideas," Missie said. "There's no number twelve listed here."

"Good," Willie said. "Then I won't be breakin' a rule when I kiss ya." He pulled Missie into his arms.

Missie fought to keep her tears from coming as Willie held her close. She was glad that Willie did not release her right away. It gave her time to regain her composure. At last she stepped back and smiled.

"I'll bet if she'd thought of it, that would have been on the list," she said. Willie grinned and kissed her again.

Willie and Missie went downstairs and promptly settled the account. Missie could have cried as she watched him pay for three and a half long months. How could she ever bear it? She would die of lonesomeness. She turned her back and bit her lips in an effort to keep herself under control.

Mrs. Taylorson tucked the money in the bosom of her dress and smiled at the couple.

Mrs. Taylorson insisted that Missie move in right away. The day would be spent in sorting out what Missie would need and getting her settled. There was no rule about sewing machines, but just to be safe, Missie asked concerning hers. She was pleased that Mrs. Taylorson did not object to having hers in the room. Missie would enjoy her machine and the hours that she could spend sewing for her coming baby.

In order to lose no time, Mrs. Taylorson informed them that they would be expected for the evening meal at 6:00 sharp. She would see them then. If they needed assistance in the meantime, they could feel free to knock on the kitchen door.

Willie drove their wagon down the dusty street that ran in front of the Taylorsons' home and the sorting began. It was hard to decide what should go and what should stay. Missie tended to want to send everything, and Willie kept thinking of things that she might need or long for. At last they reached a compromise and Missie was soon settled in. Willie, too, moved in his few needs for the one week that he would share the room with Missie. He then returned the wagon to the outskirts of the town where it was left in Henry's care.

Promptly at six the LaHayes descended the steps toward the hall, hoping that it would not be too difficult to find the dining room. It wasn't; the aroma of food guided them. They entered the room and found the table set for four.

A gentleman was already seated, fork in hand, but he did have the courtesy to lay down his fork and rise to his feet as the couple entered. It wasn't exactly a smile that crossed his face to welcome them, but neither was it a frown.

"Howdya do," he said officiously, extending a hand to Willie. "I'm J. B. Taylorson."

Missie wondered what the J. B. was for.

"I'm William LaHaye—an' this is my wife Melissa," Willie responded. Missie almost snickered.

Mr. Taylorson nodded to the chairs, "Won't ya sit down." It was plain that he wanted to get on with the business of eating.

Willie seated Missie and took the chair beside her, just as Mrs. Taylorson entered from the kitchen with a dish of food in each hand.

"Here ya are," she said. "I told Ben thet I told ya six sharp."

So the "B" was for Ben. That still left the "J."

Mrs. Taylorson settled herself and Mr. Taylorson blessed the food. He said the prayer in the same manner that he said his "howdy"—as though it were a demanded courtesy that he had no power to avoid. Once it was over, his full attention was given to the meal. The beans, potatoes and meat were simple, yet tasty, and very welcome after the monotonous trail fare.

Mrs. Taylorson allowed no slack in the conversation. Her questions followed so closely on the heels of one another that there was scarcely time for a civil reply. She offered many suggestions as to what a mother-to-be should be eating and doing, and most of them made a lot of sense. Willie felt great inward relief to know that Missie would be well cared for.

After the meal was over, Mr. Taylorson slid back his chair and pulled a pipe from his pocket.

"Now, Ben," Mrs. Taylorson chided, "smoke's not good fer a woman in Mrs. LaHaye's condition. Why don't ya take thet on out to the porch?"

Missie felt embarrassed. "That's fine, Mrs. Taylorson. We don't want to drive your husband from his own home. Willie and I were thinkin' of a walk, anyway."

But Mr. Taylorson rose.

"I'd rather smoke on the porch enyhow—git out of this insufferable heat." He gathered his pipe and tobacco and headed for the door. "You smoke?" he asked Willie.

"No, sir."

"Ya can join me enyway iffen you'd like."

Willie followed him out and Missie began to help Mrs. Taylorson clear the table.

"Now, now," Mrs. Taylorson said in alarm. "Yer board and room payment doesn't say anything 'bout deductions fer yer help."

Missie stammered, "I—I wasn't thinkin' of deductions. I just thought that I could give you a hand."

"Fine—fine, iffen ya wish to, but it ain't called fer—an' it won't change a thing."

Missie helped carry the leftover food and the dishes to the kitchen. It really was unbearably hot. She finally excused herself and went to find Willie. She really did want a walk.

Chapter 18

News

Two days later, amid the busyness of getting ready to leave with the southbound supply train, Willie burst through the bedroom door. Missie had been at her sewing.

"Guess what?" he exclaimed, hardly able to contain himself.

"Whatever it be, it must really be somethin'," Missie answered with puzzled surprise.

"It is! It really is! I went in to thet tely-graph place up town and I found out thet fer only a few cents we can send a telygram back home."

"Back home?"

"Yep! Right to yer folks. The office in town there will git the message to 'em. So I figured as how we should do jest that."

"What would we say?"

"Jest let 'em know thet we made it safe an' sound—an'—maybe tell 'em about the baby."

"Oh, Willie," Missie cried, "could we?"

"Grab whatever ya need an' let's go."

Missie quickly smoothed her hair, then picked up a light

cotton bonnet. Just in time she remembered the window and gently closed it just in case Mrs. Taylorson should check her room while she was gone. Willie had to restrain Missie's pace on the way to the telegraph office.

"Slow down some. It ain't gonna go away," he said with a laugh. Then he continued, "The man says thet ya have ten words."

"Oh, dear," Missie sighed, "how are we gonna say it all in ten words?"

They reached the office, and Willie opened the door for Missie. She didn't know if her breathlessness was due to their brisk walk or her excitement.

They labored together over the wording, composing and changing, re-composing and changing again. Finally they felt that they had done the best that they could. Willie handed the message and the money to the man behind the desk.

The message read, "Isaiah 41:10. Missie remains, Tettsford. Grandchild due October. Inform Pa."

Missie's eyes misted as she envisioned the excitement and relief when the telegram was received by her parents and the news was passed on to Willie's pa.

"Oh, Willie," Missie asked, "do ya think Pa LaHaye will mind gettin' the message secondhand?"

"Iffen I know my pa," Willie said, "he'd think me a squanderin' ignoramous iffen I sent two of 'em to the same town."

"When will it get there?"

"Fella says if no lines are down and there's no other trouble, they should have it in a coupl'a days.

"Now I'll walk ya on back to Taylorsons and then git back to the figurin' an' loadin' of my supplies."

"No need to go with me. I'll find my way back and just sorta take my time. Where's Henry?"

"He's over at the smithy's. He's been a powerful help to me. I don't know what I'd a-done without 'im."

"Has he been callin' again?"

"Iffen ya mean has he been to town, yes. I haven't asked him his doin's."

Missie smiled. "It's not really that hard to figure though, is it?"

"Poor Henry," said Willie, "he has my sympathy. Once one of you cute little things git yer fingers all twisted up in a fella's heart, he's a goner. Well, I'll see ya at six."

Missie turned to walk back to the Taylorsons, lighthearted in spite of the oppressive heat.

She tried again to picture her pa and ma when they'd read the telegram. It wasn't hard to figure what they'd do. They'd stop whatever they were doing and thank God for His care for their children, and they would pray for the new baby. Missie felt both joy and sadness together.

When she reached her room she was no longer in the mood for sewing. She opened her window wide and lay down on the bed.

In a very few days the supply train would be going south, with Willie following. How she wished she could go as well. The absurd notion of trying to stow away crossed her mind. Willie would only turn around and bring her back once he discovered her. No, there seemed no way out. Willie would go and she would have to stay.

"God," she prayed, "that help you're a-promisin'—I'm really gonna need it now." The tears were again threatening to come when Missie heard steps on the stairs. She quickly went to the window and closed it.

"Ya got visitors," Mrs. Taylorson called. "Seein' as how they be ladies, I gave 'em the privilege of the parlor."

Missie hurried down. To her joy she found Kathy Weiss and Melinda Emory.

She greeted them eagerly, exchanging a quick hug with each girl by turn.

"Henry told us where to find ya," Kathy explained.

"Oh, I'm so glad that you came," Missie said. "I was up in my room lying down, and beginning to feel sorry for myself."

Mrs. Emory took her hand. "An' you have reason to, Mrs. LaHaye. If I were you, I'd be feeling the same way."

"Would you?"

Melinda Emory nodded her head and tears showed in her eyes. "I would. In fact I'm not sure that I would stand for it at all."

"Oh, I tried to argue, but Willie just wouldn't hear of it. He's downright unreasonable 'bout it—since Becky."

"I can understand how Willie feels," Kathy said. "An' as hard as it is, I think he might be right."

" 'Course he is," Melinda said. "Men *usually* are. It's just very difficult for us women, that's all. We're too sentimental to be practical."

Missie nodded. "I guess that's so," she said, "an' I'm afraid that I have made it rather hard for Willie."

"I don't suppose he expected you to stay without *some* resistance."

Melinda, changing the subject, then asked, "Are you all settled?"

"Yes—I guess so. I kept as few things as I could so that it wouldn't mean too much trouble later. I did keep my sewing machine. Willie thought it would help me to be busy—and I do need to do the sewin' for the baby. Anyway, I love to sew."

"So do I," Melinda said with fervor. "I had a machine—" She stopped short.

Missie quickly spoke up, "Oh, if you'd like to use my machine—anytime. I would be so pleased to have your company."

"Could I?"

"Please do! The little bit of sewing that I have to do will never keep me busy for the whole three months."

Melinda smiled. "Thank you so much, Mrs. LaHaye. I would so appreciate that."

"Please, call me Missie."

"An' my name is Melinda. You can even shorten it if you like."

"Melinda suits you. I like it."

Melinda smiled.

"I heard you found work," Missie continued.

"Yes, of a sort."

"It must be awfully tiring."

"It is that, but at least I'm paying my own way and it won't be long until school starts. With my salary from the hotel—an' your sewin' machine—perhaps I can start school in style." She smiled again.

"I was a schoolteacher, too—before I married Willie."

"Really? An' a good one, I'm sure."

"I hope so. At any rate, I loved it. Some days I miss it."

"I wish I had some trainin' like thet," Kathy remarked. "I'd love to git a job to help Pa out fer awhile. But the only work thet is available fer a girl here, iffen she doesn't have special trainin'—well, Pa won't hear tell of."

"Your pa will make out just fine, I'm sure," Melinda comforted. "In no time at all he'll have all the business that he can handle."

Kathy smiled a weak, yet hopeful, smile. "Yeah, I reckon he will. Still, I'd like to do more than just keep house."

"Do you like to sew?" asked Missie.

"I've never learned, so I really don't know."

"Well, why don't I teach you? Between Melinda and you and me, we'll really keep my machine hummin'."

They all laughed.

"Could ya? I mean, would ya mind?"

" 'Course not, I'd love to."

"Then I'd love it too."

Mrs. Taylorson bustled through the door.

"I brung you girls some tea," she said. "Company don't come to my house an' not git served—even iffen it ain't my company."

"Oh, Mrs. Taylorson, how kind!" Missie exclaimed, pleased that her landlady was so thoughtful. She introduced her friends and explained to Mrs. Taylorson that she might see them often. Mrs. Taylorson seemed to enjoy the idea. It occurred to Missie that the woman might not have much company of her own and missed it.

The girls continued their visit over their tea and cookies, including Mrs. Taylorson in their conversation.

At length the visitors rose to leave. They invited Missie to visit them, which she promised to do.

Mrs. Taylorson eagerly invited the girls to return "jest anytime." Missie returned to her room feeling much better. It had been a good day. God had given the help He'd promised. The telegram home, the visit with friends—a reminder that she would not really be alone when Willie left—these were gentle kindnesses given from the hand of a loving Father. With all of these blessings, Missie felt a warm glow inside.

But then she thought of Willie's impending departure, and the warm glow faded somewhat.

Her thoughts were interrupted by a noise on the stairs. She turned to the door. Willie entered the room and deposited a strange heap on the floor. To Missie it looked like a bundle of canvas.

"What's that?" she asked, pointing.

"The gear thet I'll be needin'."

"Gear?"

"Fer ridin', once I'm at the ranch."

"You're gonna ride in *that*?"

"Sure am. It might look a bit strange, but it's a cowboy's best friend out on the range."

"What is it," Missie asked skeptically, "an' how do you use it?"

Willie lifted the canvas. "It's chaps," he explained. "Ya jest pull 'em on over yer trousers, like so. The heavy canvas sheds the rain, takes the spines of the cactus and keeps all manner of weather and injury from a rider. Ya really ought to have some yerself."

Missie laughed, and then pointed to a square of red material. "An' what's that?" she asked.

"A bandana. Ya wear it round yer neck—tied loosely like this." Willie demonstrated. "When ya get drivin' them little dogies an' the dust flies so thet ya can hardly breathe, ya just pull it up over yer mouth an' nose—like this!"

Missie giggled. "I thought that was what you used when you were holdin' up a bank."

"Guess a few have used it fer thet as well," Willie smiled. "I'll remember thet, should I ever intend to hold up a bank."

Missie laughed again and then turned seriously for a good look at the strange apparel. It was going to take some getting used to—seeing Willie decked out in these strange canvas pants. She tried to imagine herself in them and smiled softly.

"Reckon for now," she said, "I'll just plan to fight the cactus an' the rain without the help of those."

Chapter 19

Sunday

The week passed quickly, and it was Sunday. After inquiring the time of service, Willie and Missie prepared themselves and headed for the church spire they had seen. The building was bare and drab on the outside, but inside it showed evidence that someone cared for it. The congregation was small, even though the numbers were boosted some by the presence of Henry, Mr. Weiss and Kathy, Melinda Emory and the LaHayes.

The preacher looked old and rather worn-out, Missie thought, but when he arose to preach, fire was in his voice and his face glowed; Missie was caught up in his sermon. It was so good to hear real preaching again. She had enjoyed the services of the wagon train, but she had missed having a preacher speak from the Word of God.

The preacher greeted each one kindly at the door and expressed a welcome to the newcomers, inviting them back. Willie explained to the man that he would not be around for another Sunday but he was sure that Missie would be there faithfully.

"We shall welcome you," the old gentleman said with

warmth. "And if you should ever need a friend, my wife and I would be happy to welcome you to our home, as well."

Missie thanked him for his kindness and stepped out into the shimmering day.

"Anything you'd be a-carin' to do today?" Willie asked as they walked the short distance back to the Taylorsons.

"Yeah," said Missie, with longing in her voice, "I'd like to go for a long walk among some cool trees, or picnic beside a crik, or maybe just lay beside a spring and watch the water gurgle."

"Missie," pleaded Willie, "don't—please, don't."

"I'm sorry," Missie whispered. She tried hard to think of something that could actually be done and enjoyed in the heat of this dusty, drab town.

"We could call on the Weisses."

"All right," Willie agreed enthusiastically, relieved that she had thought of something. "I sure do hope thet Henry won't think I'm spyin' on 'im." He caught her hand in his.

That afternoon at the Weisses, they received such a hearty welcome that Missie's spirits lifted. Henry also was there, though he didn't seem one bit put out to have his boss appear. Melinda Emory was there, too, so the six of them settled in for a good visit. Kathy served cold tea, declaring the day to be far too warm for hot tea or coffee.

Missie was surprised at how quickly the time flew by.

"Can ya stay fer supper?" Kathy pleaded.

"Oh, I don't think we can," Missie said. "We didn't say anything to Mrs. Taylorson, an' supper is at six."

She and Willie exchanged smiles.

"How 'bout iffen I run over an' inform yer good landlady?" Henry asked.

"Oh, but—"

"Why not?"

"Please stay," Kathy begged. "The men will be gone by next Sunday."

Missie weakened. "Well, I'm not sure what she'll think, but—well—okay. Iffen she hasn't started to prepare, she shouldn't mind, should she?"

It turned out that both Henry and Willie walked over

together while the girls went to the kitchen to give Kathy a hand.

Mrs. Taylorson did not object. In fact, Willie got the impression that she was relieved at not having to fuss about for extras on such a warm day.

Kathy's meal consisted of fried meat, hot biscuits and gravy. It was served with love and laughter, and everyone enjoyed the time spent together.

"I know," Kathy said, after the dishes had been washed, "let's have a sing-song, for ol' times' sake."

The rest agreed. Henry went for his guitar, while Mr. Weiss tuned up his violin.

They sang all the songs that they knew—folk songs, love songs, dance tunes and hymns. When they were finished, they sang their favorite ones all over again.

It was late when Willie and Missie walked back to the Taylorsons hand in hand.

"I'm afraid that we've broken Rule Number Six," Missie said.

"An' what is thet?"

"Bedtime is at ten o'clock," Missie replied in a mock stern voice. She broke into laughter, then quickly checked herself and added, "We'd better be careful or we'll break Number Two as well."

"An' thet is—"

Missie affected a gruff, deep voice again. "No loud talkin' or laughin'."

"Ya little goose," Willie said, putting his arm around her waist and drawing her close. "Do ya have 'em all memorized by number?"

"I think so. I've read them often enough."

"Speakin' of readin'," Willie said, "ya really should have somethin' on hand to read. I'll talk to the preacher tomorrow. He may have a good idea of what books can be had."

"Oh, Willie, stop frettin' 'bout me. I've got all that sewin' to do, and all that yarn to be knitted up, a piano to learn to play, and sewin' lessons to give. Surely it will keep me busy."

"Well, we want to be sure," said Willie.

Chapter 20

Parting

On Wednesday Willie announced that the wagon train would be pulling out early the next morning. Missie had to bite her lip all evening to keep the tears from flowing. She hoped that Willie didn't notice, but of course he did. They retired to their room early so that Willie could get all of his belongings packed. It didn't take long. Time suddenly seemed to be heavy on their hands.

"Funny," Missie mused, "time is so short and precious, an' yet one doesn't really know how to spend it."

"Have ya everything thet ya need?" asked Willie for the umpteenth time.

"I'm sure that I have."

"Well, I'll leave ya some money, jest in case."

"Really, Willie, I don't think I'll be needin'—"

"Ya never know. Maybe somethin' thet ya need or be wantin'— an' you'll need some fer church offerin'."

Missie only nodded.

"I'm glad thet you have Kathy an' Melinda."

"Me too."

"I hope ya see 'em real often."

"Melinda will be workin'—but she promised to come over evenin's to sew."

"An' Kathy is free to come anytime—right?"

Missie nodded again. "The first thing that she wants to sew are some curtains for her kitchen window."

"An' ya can visit 'em too," continued Willie.

Missie agreed.

"Ya might pay a call on the preacher an' his wife, too. They seem like real nice folks. Jest don't stay out too late—please, Missie?"

"I won't. Promise."

"One can't be too careful."

"*You're* the one that needs to be careful. Here I am all tucked away safe in a town, where the worst that can happen to me is to get dust in my eyes—an' you're tellin *me* to be careful. It's you that's goin' to have to take care, Willie."

Willie smoothed her hair.

"Won't much happen to me. I'm travelin' south with a whole passel of supply wagons, an' Henry'll be with me once we reach our spread. No need to worry none 'bout me."

"I s'pose so," Missie admitted. "I just won't be able to keep from it, though."

"I'll worry, too," Willie said his voice husky. "It doesn't pleasure me none to leave ya, Missie. If only there was some other way."

"I'll be fine." Missie tried for Willie's sake to say the words as though she really meant them.

"Missie," Willie hesitated, holding her close. "Missie—the wagons are to pull out real early in the mornin'. I don't intend to wake ya when I leave, so this will be my good-bye tonight. I love ya. I've loved ya ever since ya were a little schoolgirl."

"An' you showed it," she whispered, "by dunkin my hair ribbons in an inkwell."

"An' carvin' our initials—"

"An puttin' a grasshopper in my lunchpail."

"An' tellin' young Todd Culver thet I'd knock out his teeth

iffen he didn't leave my girl alone; an' closin' yer classroom window when it got stuck; an' prayin' fer ya every single day—thet iffen God willed, ya'd learn to love me."

"You did that?"

"I did."

"Oh, Willie," Missie sobbed, pressing her face against him. "I'll miss ya so—so much."

When Missie awoke the next morning, she was alone in her bed, and Willie's things were gone from the room. An emptiness filled her that she could not have put into words; she turned into her pillow and sobbed. How would she ever cope? She missed him so already. She had promised herself secretly the night before that she would be sure to waken so that she might feel the comfort of Willie's arms once more. She felt annoyed at herself for failing to awaken; yet she had to admit that it would not have made it any easier to say good-bye again.

If only I was at home with Mama and Pa to console me. . . . They would understand about pain and separation. She recalled Willie's words when Melinda was grieving: "Yer ma an' pa knew such grief."

They had—and they had lived through it. And she could too. After all, Willie *would* be coming back. The wait wouldn't be so long—not really.

She forced herself to crawl out of bed, then bathed her face at the basin. She caught herself wondering if this was wash Number One or Two for this water, and if she could now throw it out and get some fresh. Her eyes moved to Mrs. Taylorson's list. The empty space for number twelve now had some writing beside it. Had Mrs. Taylorson come up with another rule? Missie crossed the room for a better look, and read Number Twelve aloud: "Number Twelve, Always remember that I love you—both of you."

"Oh, Willie, ya silly goose!" she cried as tears streamed down her freshly washed cheeks. She was going to have to wash her face again before going down for breakfast. That, for sure, would entitle her to some fresh water.

Chapter 21

Putting in Time

Missie put her mind to settling in for the long stay alone.
First, she sat down and listed all of the "must-do's" on a piece of
paper. Then she listed all the "want-to-do's." Neither list
seemed very long. How would those tasks ever keep her occupied
until she was free to leave this town? She laid the list aside and
went to her sewing material.

She spread out all the fabric she had purchased and drew up a
tentative plan of just what she would sew from each piece. She
then checked her yarn and listed the articles that she would knit
or crochet. She laid that list aside as well and took a fresh sheet of
paper. This would be her weekly visitation list—one call each per
week on Kathy and Melinda and at least one call *from* them in
return to use Missie's machine. She placed that list with the
others and took still another sheet of paper.

She sketched out a week with a space for each hour of the day
and filled in her proposed activities: sewing, sewing lessons, knitting, laundry, reading, visits, shopping (she didn't know what
for, but it filled a space and the walk would do her good); she

even included time spent at the piano in an effort to learn to play a bit. Her week still had many vacant hours and she didn't see how she could stretch out her planned activities to fill them.

She then juggled, rearranged and stretched all that she could. Finally, she filled in all the extra spots with the words "free time" and tried to convince herself that somehow "free time" should be cherished as a special liberty.

She had scheduled sewing for her first morning, so she began on a small blanket. As simple as the job was, she just couldn't keep her mind on it, so she laid it aside and tried to read one of the books the preacher had kindly lent her. After trying to read the first page three times, unable to concentrate, she tossed it on the bed.

"It's just no use," she muttered, grabbing up some knitting. "I just can't think clear!"

She had added only a few stitches to the sock that she was making, when Mrs. Taylorson called up the stairs.

"Ya have a caller, Miss."

Missie so wished that Mrs. Taylorson wouldn't call her "Miss," as though she were still a young girl instead of a grown married woman!

It was Kathy who had come to call. Missie almost cried with relief at seeing her friend so soon after the men had left.

"Did you come to sew the curtains?" she asked.

"Goodness, no! I don't think thet I could concentrate on sewin' anythin' today. I jest had to git out fer awhile, an' I thought thet maybe you'd be a needin' it as well."

"You're absolutely right," Missie said emphatically. "Just let me get my bonnet."

The girls strolled through the streets of the dusty town, window-shopping and talking. Occasionally they entered a store, just to look around. Neither of them purchased a thing, but Missie returned home in better spirits, and Kathy promised to come over that very evening for her first sewing lesson.

In the afternoon, Missie sat down and made herself a calendar. She marked each day's date in big numbers, wrote Willie's name beside the first one, August 2, then circled October 25—it was as close as she could figure the baby's arrival date to be. In between the two dates stretched many seemingly empty days, but Missie intended to strike them off, one by one, in hopes that they would go quickly.

It was warm in the room, and Missie was feeling emotionally and physically exhausted, so she kicked off her shoes and stretched out on the bed to rest.

"It all will be worth it," she told herself. "By the time Willie comes for me and the baby, he'll have our house ready. I'll be able to move right in, 'stead of livin' cramped in that stuffy old wagon. Just think—our own home! I'll hang up the curtains that Mama helped me sew, spread out the cozy rugs, make up the bed with all those warm quilts. I'll put my dishes in the cupboards, set up the sewin' machine, put all the crocks an' barrels in my pantry—all those things that a woman be a-needin' in her own home."

She let the happy thoughts drive away the threatening tears and drifted off to sleep.

Kathy came that evening as promised. She was a little slow at catching on to the rhythm of the foot treadle having never used a sewing machine before, but eventually she had a good start on the curtains.

Day One was finally over. Missie crossed it off her new calendar with relief, and knelt beside her bed. Somewhere out there, in the dark, distant night, she knew that Willie would be remembering her in prayer as well. It helped to ease her loneliness.

At the end of each plodding day, Missie struck the numbers from the calendar in the manner of a general triumphant after battle. She had survived her first Sunday alone, her first hairwashing, and her first washday. She was working on her third day at the piano when Mrs. Taylorson called, "Miss, ya have a feller here with a telygram."

Missie fairly flew to the door. What news could be so important that it needed to reach her by telegram? Her heart thumped wildly within her, every beat crying, "Willie! Willie!" She accepted the telegram with a shaking hand and quickly scanned the small sheet.

"Received message—Stop—Praise God—Stop—Happy and concerned about baby—Stop—Isaiah"

"Mama and Pa!" she exclaimed, and to the waiting Mrs. Taylorson: "It's from my folks—they've just acknowledged our message."

Missie smiled through her tears and hurried up the stairs to her room. Once inside, with the door closed behind her, she crushed the blessed message to her breast and fell to her knees beside her bed, the tears falling unashamedly.

"Oh, Mama—Pa—I miss you both so much, and I love you so . . . Oh—if only. . . ."

Missie posted the telegram beneath Willie's Rule Number Twelve. Many times a day she would read it and think of the dear people who had sent it to her.

As the days decreased on Missie's calendar, her pile of sewn articles and knitted things increased. Kathy had come often, and soon progressed to sewing dresses when the curtains and some aprons were finished.

Melinda also had spent evenings with Missie. Her job in the hotel kitchen had been very taxing on her limited strength, so she never was able to stay very late. But she had managed, with her small income, to buy yard goods for three attractive dresses, and sew them for use in the schoolroom. Her days as restaurant cook and dishwasher were over at last, and she was happily employed as the town's new schoolmarm.

Missie twice had called on the preacher and his wife. She not only found their company very refreshing but they also returned each call. Mrs. Taylorson was quite beside herself to have a parson in her parlor.

After Missie had prepared for bed one night, she stood studying her calendar. It was now September 8.

"September 8 is a long way from the second of August," she whispered to herself. "Not halfway yet, but almost—almost." She made a long black mark through the number and went to kneel beside her bed. As she was praying, she heard a gentle rapping on her door. Missie looked up in surprise. She hadn't heard anyone on the stairs.

Then the door opened, and there stood Willie. Paralyzed with shock, Missie remained on her knees and just stared.

Not one to wait for her bidding, he quickly bent down and whisked her to her feet.

"It's really you!" Missie gasped incredulously. "It's really you!" And then she was in his arms, clinging to him, sobbing into his jacket while he showered kisses on her face and rocked her gently back and forth.

"I jest couldn't stand it anymore," he said huskily.

"You came for me?"

"Oh, no," Willie corrected her hurriedly. "Just to *see* you, thet's all. I was jest so lonesome thet Henry finally said, 'Why don't ya jest make yerself a little trip? Ya ain't rightly of much use here anyway. So I did."

"Where's Henry?"

"I left him workin' on the corrals."

Missie laughed then. "Don't know how you ever got away to come here without Henry. Why, he must be near as lonesome as you."

"He did send a couple of letters with me—*three*, in fact. He sent you one, too."

Missie laughed again.

"Dear ol' Henry—an' he sent *two* others?"

"Yep. One to the Weisses and one to Melinda."

"He's just writing *all* his friends."

"But I want to hear 'bout *you*," Willie said firmly. "How ya been?"

"Lonesome!" Missie said, threatening to burst into tears again.

"Me, too," Willie replied. "Me too." And he kissed her again.

"How long can you stay?"

"Just till day after tomorrow."

"Only one day?" Missie's face crumpled.

Willie nodded. "I gotta git back, Missie. I shouldn'ta come, really. We've got so much to do 'fore winter sets in, but—well, I jest couldn't stay away. I've gotta leave mornin' after next."

"Do you have a house?"

"A temporary one—that's the way most folks do. Then they build later—as they can."

"And the cattle?"

"Only a few head. We can't really take on too many until we're ready for 'em, an' then ya need men to care for 'em too. After that ya need a bunkhouse to bed the men."

"How many men?"

"Four or five at first."

"Ya mean I'm gonna be cookin' for six or seven men?" Missie was flabbergasted.

"No, silly." Willie pulled her back against him. "The cook does thet in the cookshack."

"You gotta have a cookshack, too?"

"Yeah, an' we hafta git all thet ready this fall."

Missie took his hand and they sat down on the edge of the bed.

"Didn't realize that it took that many men to run a ranch," she said thoughtfully.

"Should rightly have more than that, but I'm gonna try to make do fer the time bein'."

"What on earth do they all do?"

"Need shifts fer one thing. Always should be some of 'em out there ridin' herd on things—watchin' the cattle an' watchin' fer trouble."

"Trouble—you mean like wild animals an' such?"

"S'pose wild animals enter into it—but they're not the greatest danger."

"What, then?"

Willie grinned. "Accordin' to what I hear, a rancher's biggest threat comes from *tame animals.*"

"Meanin'?"

"Rustlers."

"Rustlers?"

"Yep. More than one rancher has been driven from the land—forced to give up an' move on out, because of rustlers."

"That's horrible!" Missie exclaimed. "They carry guns?"

"Reckon they do," Willie said calmly.

"But what do we do?" Missie would not let the matter drop. "Will you order your men to carry guns?"

"My men don't need those orders. They're used to havin' a gun hangin' from their saddle."

"But—but, would they *kill* someone?" Missie could hardly force the word out.

"My men have orders never to shoot to kill another human bein'," Willie said firmly, "even iffen it means losin' the whole herd."

"Might they do that—the rustlers I mean? Might they take the whole herd?"

"Not usually. They normally just drive off a few at a time— pickin' on stragglers, gradually workin' at a herd—especially one that isn't carefully watched. Sometimes their need—or their greed—drives 'em to make a bold move and try fer the entire lot."

"Oh, Willie, what will we do if—"

"Now let's not borrow trouble," Willie said. "We'll hire the men thet we can and protect the herd the best thet we can. Thet's all we can do."

"But how can you afford to pay all those men?"

" 'Fraid a cowboy don't make all thet much. Nice fer ranchers, but not so great fer the cowboys. They do git their bed and board and enough money to buy the tobacco and few supplies thet they be needin'. Some even manage to lay a little aside. As to the payin' of 'em, I figured thet in my accounts when I was workin' out what we'd be needin'. When we start sellin' cattle of our own, their wages will come from the sales."

Missie felt relieved to know that Willie had things well under control.

"What else do they do?" she asked, getting back to the cowboys.

"Break horses, build and fix fences, watch fer sickness an' snakes an' varmints. They care for the critters during bad storms an' keep an eye on the pasture and water holes to make sure thet the cows are well cared for. Their main job, though, is to keep the cows grazin' well together so thet there ain't alot of stragglers scattered through the hills—easy victims of prowlin' animals an' rustlers."

"Sounds like a big job to me."

"Is a big job. But most cowboys wouldn't trade it fer any other job in the world."

"Let's forget cowboys, cookshacks and bunkhouses," Missie interrupted. "Let's think 'bout us for awhile."

Willie agreed as his arm tightened around her.

"Yer lookin' good. Feelin' okay?"

"Oh, Willie!" Missie suddenly burst out, ignoring his question. "I forgot to show you. Look!"

She jumped up and pointed to the telegram on her wall.

"Mama and Pa got our message," she continued, "an' they sent one of their own!"

Willie grinned as he stood to read the telegram.

"Makes 'em seem a lot closer-like, don't it?"

Missie nodded.

"This trip made you seem closer, too," said Willie. "Took six days to make it down there by wagon—but I made it in 'bout half the time on horseback."

"You did? Then it's really not so *awful* far, is it?" Missie was comforted.

Willie left as the sun edged over the horizon. He had spent two nights with Missie. She wondered if she could face the dreadful agonies of parting again—but it was not as difficult as she had feared. She struck two more days from her calendar as she went to bed that night. She had completely forgotten it during Willie's visit.

Chapter 22

The New Baby

Missie was restless. The book that she had attempted to read lay discarded on her pillow. Her sewing projects were completed; she wasn't about to buy more fabric for things that she really could do without. She had run out of yarn, but had no desire to make a trip to the store for more—though certain that she could put it to good use. Maybe a visit to Kathy's . . . no, her heart wasn't in it.

Listless, edgy, and out of sorts, she paced her room—back and forth. Was it the heat, or was she just tired? When it was twelve-thirty, *sharp*—time for the noon meal—she knew that she wasn't hungry. She called down to Mrs. Taylorson that she didn't feel like eating—could she please be excused? She'd just lie down awhile.

She hadn't been down for long when a sudden contraction tightened her abdomen. To her relief, it soon subsided. Missie closed her eyes and tried to sleep, but before she could drop off, another one shuddered through her.

When this passed, Missie sat up and squinted at her homemade calendar on the wall. "It can't be," she said. "This is only the tenth. You can't come yet, Baby. It just isn't time! It *can't* be!" But Missie soon realized that it was indeed time.

She climbed out of bed and paced for awhile, then lay down, only to get up and pace some more.

What will Willie think? I told him October twenty-fifth—an' he said he'd be here on the twenty-second, just to be sure. Maybe I'm just imaginin', or maybe it's just a false alarm.

But it was not a false alarm. Missie's landlady soon recognized it for what it really was, even though she had never had children of her own. She suggested sending immediately for the doctor, but Missie insisted on waiting. At last Mrs. Taylorson could stand it no more. She sent Mr. Taylorson over for the doctor before the good man could even enjoy his after-supper pipe. To Missie's relief, the doctor was not off tending a gunshot wound or setting a broken bone, and came almost at once.

That night, about 10 o'clock, a son was born to Missie—two weeks early by her calculations. He was not big, but he was healthy and strong. His young mother, who had been repeating over and over, throughout her time of delivery, "Fear thou not, for I am with thee," cried tears of joy at her first sight of him.

After the doctor had gone, and Missie and the baby were bedded for the night, Mrs. Taylorson still waddled about the room, clucking and fussing like a mother hen.

"He's a dandy little wee'un, ain't he? What ya gonna call 'im?"

"I don't know," Missie replied sleepily. "I tried to talk of names with Willie—but he said he'd be here when the baby arrived an' we'd pick a name then."

"But he ain't comin' fer two weeks yet," said the practical Mrs. Taylorson. "Don't seem fittin' thet a child should go fer two whole weeks without a name."

"I know," Missie said, smiling at her son who lay snuggled up against her. "I guess I'll have to name 'im."

"Ya got a name picked?"

"One I like. I just *happened* to marry a man with the same middle name as my pa. Now doesn't it seem fittin' that my son should bear that name?"

"Deed it do!" Mrs. Taylorson exclaimed. "Yer Willie could hardly fault ya on thet choice. What's the name?"

"Nathan," said Missie. "Nathan." She said it again, savoring the sound of it.

"Nathan?" Mrs. Taylorson repeated. "Rather nice. I like it. I think it even suits the wee package. Nathan—jest Nathan?"

"No, Nathan *Isaiah*."

"Isaiah?" Mrs. Taylorson looked a bit doubtful on this one, but she made no comment concerning Missie's choice. "Is Isaiah somethin' special, too?"

"It certainly is," Missie said with tears in her eyes. "Very special."

Missie pulled the covers about herself and her small son. She was so happy—and so tired. She kissed the fuzzy top of Nathan's head and let her body relax. She had almost dozed off when a sudden thought hit her.

"Mrs. Taylorson," she said sleepily, "would you be so kind as to have a telegram sent to my folks tomorrow?"

"Certainly, Miss," the woman replied. "What would ya be wantin' it to say?" She then took the paper and pencil from the desk and handed it to Missie. "Better write it down, in case I forget."

Missie thought for a few moments, then began to write slowly: "Nathan Isaiah arrived safely October 10. Love from Missie and Baby." She handed the sheet to Mrs. Taylorson.

"It would pleasure me to be the bearer of such good news."

Missie smiled ruefully at the small bundle snuggled beside her. "If only there was some way to let his pa know. I'm gonna have a powerful hard time waiting for the twenty-second. Why, Willie's son will be nigh grown-up by the time his pa gets to hold 'im!"

Mrs. Taylorson looked down at the tiny bundle on Missie's arm. "Seems to me," she smiled, "a little growin' time ain't gonna hurt the wee fella much. I don't reckon he's gonna outgrow thet little nightie he's a swimmin' in, in jest two weeks' time."

Missie smiled contentedly and let sleep claim her.

Chapter 23

Travelin' On

Willie drove into Tettsford Junction with the wagon on October twentieth, prepared for as many days of waiting as was necessary before welcoming his child. Mrs. Taylorson let him in and managed, as promised, not to reveal the household's wonderful news. Willie went on up to Missie's room.

Missie was standing at her window looking wistfully out over the back garden at the distant hills. She was even more restless now that she was on her feet again; the days seemed to take forever to pass.

Nathan, at this stage, seemed content to eat and sleep—and grow—daily, though he hadn't managed yet to fill out his nightie, just as Mrs. Taylorson had predicted.

At the sound of the door Missie did not even turn around. She had become accustomed to Mrs. Taylorson using any excuse to come in and out of the room. If she wasn't bringing Missie tea with lots of milk, she came just to check on the baby.

At Willie's alarmed, "What happened?" Missie whirled around.

"Willie!" she squealed.

He seemed paralyzed. "What's happened?" he repeated with fear in his voice.

"What do you mean, what's *happened*?"

Speechless, Willie gestured to Missie's trim figure, and she finally realized why his face had gone white.

A smile spread over her face, as she fell into his arms.

"You're a pa! That's what's happened."

"Already?"

"He fooled us, didn't he?"

"*He?*"

"Look!"

Missie grasped Willie's hand and led him to the foot of the bed where the small bundle lay peacefully sleeping in a simple cradle made by Mr. Weiss. One fist curled gently beside Nathan's full cheeks.

"Ours?" Willie whispered in awe.

"Ours," Missie said. "Isn't he somethin'?"

"Can we—can we git 'im out of there?" Willie asked swallowing hard and blinking back tears. Missie nodded. Willie bent down and carefully picked up his son.

"Isn't he somethin'," he repeated Missie's words.

Missie felt bubbly. Willie was here. Willie was pleased with his son—her gift to him. She reached up and kissed her husband's cheek.

"I think he looks like his pa," she whispered. "Look, he's gonna have dark hair. Oh, I know he'll likely lose all the baby fuzz, but I think when it comes in again, it'll be dark like yours. An' wait until he opens his eyes. They're blue now, but a dark, and hazy blue. I'm thinkin' that before long they're gonna be as brown as his pa's. But just look at this." Missie's voice held a hint of amazement and joy. She reached out one finger and gently touched young Nathan on his soft chin. "A dimple! A dimple just like yours."

She expected a protest, but instead Willie looked at the small dimple and a light began to shine in his eyes.

"Aw, c'mon," he said with a grin.

"When did he arrive?"

"October the tenth."

"The *tenth?* That's way early."

"He's almost two weeks old already—and ready to travel."

"Yer sure?"

"Doc says iffen we take it easy, we should be able to go most anytime."

Willie was too moved to speak.

"It won't take long, will it—to be ready to go?" Missie asked.

"No—no, not long. I'll git right on it. Henry came with me this time. We brought two teams, so's we would have plenty of room fer supplies and not have to crowd ya none." He laughed. "Henry's gonna be a heap disappointed. We was all set fer a month-long stay."

Missie laughed quietly.

"Oh, Willie. I can hardly wait. I'm so tired of being alone in this ol' town. I've been so lonesome."

The baby stirred and Willie adjusted him in his arms.

"Hey," Willie said suddenly. "Has he got a name?"

"He has." Missie assured him, "An' a good one too. He's Nathan—Nathan Isaiah."

"Nathan Isaiah," Willie repeated. "I like it." Lifting his small son up so that he could plant a kiss on his downy head, he whispered, "Nathan Isaiah, I love you."

After four days, they were ready to leave. Mrs. Taylorson could hardly bear to see them go. She cooed and cuddled the baby and insisted upon holding him until the very last moment. Even Mr. Taylorson took time off from his store to come and see them off. He reminded them three times to consider their home as their own, should they be back in town.

Kathy and Melinda were both tearful. The kind old preacher offered a parting prayer, and his wife insisted that they have some of her fresh-baked bread for the trail.

Henry fussed over Missie's bed in the wagon, determined that no wind or rain should be allowed to bring discomfort to her or the baby. It was not so hot for traveling now. In fact, Missie had to bundle up against a cool breeze.

At last they were on the trail, and Missie mentally ticked off the *new* calendar that she carried in her head. In just six days they would be *home*. Finally she would see the land that Willie had learned to love. Her excitement grew within her until she could hardly contain it. At last she would be free of the drab, barren, dusty town. She would move into her own home like a nesting bird, and make their dreams come true. She cradled her son close to her. "An' you—you little rascal," she crooned to him, "you weren't even in those dreams. But I think that you're gonna fit in just fine."

Chapter 24

The Ranch

"We're almost there now," Willie announced with excitement in his voice. "Jest over thet there next hill."

They had already traveled six days. For fear of tiring Missie or the baby, Willie had stopped each evening a little earlier than would have been normal. Now it was noon of the seventh day.

Missie swallowed hard. Just over the next hill. Could a miracle take place "just over the next hill"?

The land they had been traveling through was even more bleak than that around Tettsford Junction. Until she saw something better with her own eyes, Missie would find it impossible to believe there would be any change. Hills and more colorless hills, covered with only coarse, dry-looking grass. Tumbleweed somersaulted along in the wind, rolling and bouncing forever and ever. Occasional cactus plants or an outcropping of rocks were the only changes of scenery.

Far in the distance were the dark mountains. Missie had expected—had hoped—that the mountains would be her friends. But they remained aloof, offering only a dim outline, shadowing themselves in a gloomy haze.

"Sometimes they're purple—sometimes blue—sometimes almost pink," Willie had boasted, "dependin' on how the sun hits 'em. An' then in the winter, with the snow on their peaks, they're a dazzle of white."

"Can we see the mountains from our place?" Missie had asked, with almost a prayer that it might be so. She was so anxious to share Willie's mountains in each of their changing moods.

"Not from our valley," Willie had responded. "In order to see the mountains one would have to build up on a hill—an' ya wouldn't want thet. Too much wind, no protection."

"Too much wind," Missie muttered softly now, thinking back on Willie's words. "Way too much wind." She wrapped her heavy shawl more tightly about her.

So they couldn't see the mountains from their house. Then, what could they see? She had asked Willie that, too.

"Lookin' to the east, down the draw," Willie had said, "ya can look right out on the range. Mile after mile of low hills, with nothin' to git in the way of yer lookin'." Willie seemed to feel that the empty miles to look upon were a great asset. The thought of it made Missie shiver.

They now topped the hill and Willie reined in the horses. Missie shut her eyes wishing that she didn't have to open them.

"Well," Willie said triumphantly, "there it is. Ain't it somethin'?"

Missie opened her eyes slowly.

There it was. Tucked in a small valley, just as Willie had said, were a few small, scattered buildings and what seemed like miles and miles of corral fence.

"You said it was *green*," Missie said through stiff lips, immediately regretting the remark.

"It is in the springtime. This is late fall. Nothin's green now." Willie was unshaken. "Well, what d'ya think of it?"

Missie had been dreading that question. How could she answer it? She couldn't let Willie down—yet she couldn't lie.

"It's—it's—really somethin'," she mumbled thankful that she had remembered Willie's own words.

"Sure is," Willie agreed, interpreting her answer with his own optimism.

He pointed a finger toward the valley and leaned toward her. "The corrals for the horses and cows all lay over there."

Missie wondered how he ever thought that she or anyone else could have missed them; they seemed to fill up the whole valley.

Willie continued, "Thet there bigger buildin' is the barn— we'll build an even bigger one later. Thet there's the bunkhouse right in there, an' the cookshack is there beside it."

"Where's the house?" cut in Missie.

"The *temporary* one? Right there."

Missie's eyes followed his finger. The *temporary* house, like the bunkhouse, cookshack and barn, looked to her like a giant heap of dried grass.

"They're made of sod," Willie informed.

"Sod?"

"Yeah. Ya cut blocks of sod from the ground an' pile 'em up. Makes a real snug place to live fer the winter."

Missie swallowed, her eyes wide and heart pounding.

"Sod," she whispered. Her lips trembled as she fought to control her emotions.

Willie spoke to the team and the wagon rumbled on. Missie closed her eyes again.

No miracle had taken place "over the next hill." There was no fairyland awaiting her. But she needed a miracle now—to help her through the ordeal that she knew lay ahead.

Chapter 25

Missie's New Home

The sod house at a distance had been shock enough to behold, but Missie's close-up view of it was even more difficult. As the wagon creaked to a stop before the small, low structure, Missie caught her lip between her teeth to keep a sob from escaping.

Henry had arrived earlier, and started a fire to warm the house for the baby's entrance. He emerged now, grinning from ear to ear.

The smoke poured from the little pipe of a chimney and dissipated into the wind. Missie recognized the pungent odor of buffalo chips. They had been forced many times on the trail to use them when wood supplies had been scarce, but Missie had never really accepted or appreciated this type of fuel. As she sat on the wagon seat, she looked around and realized that there would be no wood. There were few trees in sight.

Willie helped her down and she stood a moment to steady her legs and her mind, bracing herself for whatever she found behind the dwarfed door that guarded her new home.

Willie led the way, and Missie ducked her head to follow him into the dark interior of the little sod house.

It was high noon and still the room was so dark that Missie's eyes took several moments to adjust. When she finally could see, she gazed around the one small room. In the corner stood their bed, but not the neat, spread-covered version that she had pictured it to be. It was an oversized, lumpy, quilt-covered affair definitely made up by a man.

A small black stove squatted beneath the smoke-spewing chimney. Close beside it were a small wooden table and two stools pushed beneath it. A cluttered shelf stretched along the wall; crocks and tins were randomly stacked across it.

The two windows were tiny, hardly big enough to look out of—and one had to stoop to do so.

The small panes of dirty glass were held snugly in place by the sod that was stacked firmly around them. Missie, her thoughts swirling around like leaves in a wind, promised herself that she would give them a good washing at her first opportunity. She jerked her thoughts away from the windows, amazed that at such a traumatic moment she could even notice the dirt on the tiny panes.

Her gaze traveled up to the ceiling. It, too, was sod held precariously in place by strips of board, twine and wire. It looked as if it periodically gave up parts of itself. Missie hoped that it wouldn't all come tumbling down.

She quickly lowered her eyes lest they give her away—and immediately noticed the floor. It was dirt! Just hard-packed, uneven dirt. Missie sucked in her breath but Willie was talking cheerily.

"It ain't much, but it's warm an' snug. Come next year we'll build a *real* house—of either rock or wood—ya can have yer choice."

"Coffee's ready," Henry called. Willie stepped forward to take Nathan from Missie and lay him on the bed. Missie felt reluctant to let him go but gradually released her grip. Her eyes surveyed the roof above the bed to be sure that a clump of turf was not about to fall.

"Sit right here," Henry invited, and Missie numbly did as she was told.

The hot coffee revived her somewhat, and Missie soon discovered that her hands and feet could move again. She felt Henry's eyes upon her and knew that she must respond in some way.

"Well," she said, forcing a chuckle past the lump in her throat, "sure won't be much to keepin' house."

She saw Henry's face relax. Willie reached for her hand.

"I know it won't be easy, Missie—this first year—but jest you wait. Next year, I promise, we'll build ya jest what ya want."

Missie took another swallow of coffee. Henry had brewed it strong and dark. She needed that.

"Where are all the crates an' boxes of my things?" she asked softly. She was surprised that she had said the word "my," but she couldn't have avoided it.

"We stored 'em in the back shed by the barn until ya got here. We didn't rightly know jest which stuff you'd want. I can git 'em fer ya right away, iffen you'd like."

Missie looked around her at the already crowded room.

"I think you'd best leave 'em where they be. There doesn't seem to be much room for extras here. An' Willie, put my sewin' machine with them too, will you please?"

Willie started to protest, but then his eyes also surveyed the room.

"Does seem a mite crowded-like," he said. "Funny, it seemed plumb empty when you were gone."

"Yer team is still standin' out there," Henry broke in, placing his cup on the table. "I think thet I'd best go on out an' care fer 'em. Where d'ya want the wagon left?"

"Jest pull it up beside the house. We have all the things fer this youngun to move in yet."

Henry nodded and left.

"Where's Henry stayin'?" Missie asked, toying with her cup.

"In the bunkhouse."

"Alone?"

"No, we have three others there now. Two hands an' the cook."

"Must be crowded."

"They don't have much gear."

"You've got more cattle, then?"

"A nice start."

"An' horses?"

"A fairly good string."

"You're 'bout fixed, then, I reckon."

Willie nodded, pushed his cup back and rubbed his hands wearily over his face. He stood and walked to the window, bending his head so that he could look out at whatever lay beyond.

"Missie," he said without turning around, "this was a mistake. Don't know why I didn't see it before. Jest too plumb lonesome to think straight, I guess. I never shoulda brought ya here. I shoulda left ya there at Tettsford 'til I had a decent house built. This ain't no fittin' place fer a woman—an' a baby."

Missie went silently to him, sorry that her feelings had been so conspicuous. It must have hurt Willie to see her disappointment.

"Oh, Willie," she said reaching her arms up around his neck and pulling his head down toward her, "It's all right. Truly it is. I admit, it did catch me off guard some, but I'll get used to it. Really. Really I will. I'd have never stayed there in Tettsford—not without you. I was so lonesome for ya. I near died of it every day. I'd as soon be here—no, *sooner*—I'd *sooner* be here with you than back there in that bedroom all alone."

Willie pulled her close. "Missie, I'm sorry—sorry," he whispered, "but it won't always be this way. I promise. I'll make it up to ya someday. You'll have jest as fine a place as yer own home was—as ya deserve to have."

My home! Missie thought, closing her eyes. *Oh, if only I was at home!* That was where she really belonged. Why hadn't Willie been content with it too?

She looked across at the sleeping baby and the tears stung her eyes. Willie was kissing the top of her head. If only she could keep from looking up at him, she could recover her composure. Nathan fussed, and Missie turned gently from Willie without lifting her face.

Steadying her voice she said, "He's hungry. Guess I'd better care for him before I do anything else."

"I'll bring in his things," Willie said, and reached for his hat.

"Missie." He stopped at the door and turned to her. "I love you."

She looked at him and forced a smile.

Chapter 26

Winter

Missie lifted the already heavy buckets and trudged forward a few paces. She dropped them with a thump and stooped again to gather buffalo chips from the near-frozen ground. The driving wind whipped her shawl and she made an effort to wrap it more securely about her. Her fingers tingled from the cold; she chided herself for not having worn mittens.

At length the second pail was full. She hoisted her load and hiked slowly back to her sod house, the buckets slapping against her legs. She would need two more pails to complete the day's supply. She dreaded the thought of going out once more. Her arms and back were aching and she was now having to range farther and farther from the house in order to fill her pails.

As she neared the shanty she could hear Nathan crying. She hurried her steps. Poor little fellow! How long had he been asking for his dinner?

Missie set down her pails, then scrubbed her hands thoroughly at the basin in the corner. The cold water increased the tingling feeling; she rubbed them vigorously with the rough towel in an effort to restore the proper circulation. At last there was feeling in her fingers again. Casting her shawl aside, she hurried to her baby, crooning words of love to him even before she reached his bed.

Somehow she had survived the first two long weeks of living in the crowded shanty. Nathan was part of the reason. The wee baby brought life and meaning to Missie's world.

The air was growing colder now and the wind more harsh. Willie's eyes, full of concern, often watched the sky. A winter storm of sleet and snow could sweep in upon them long before he and his farmhands were ready for it. Missie worried about her dwindling fuel supply, but she said nothing to Willie. No need to give him further concern. Surely a woman should be able to shoulder the task of keeping the fire going. Still, she didn't know how she would handle it once the snow covered the ground. Worry nagged constantly in the back of her mind.

She changed Nathan, fed him, and held him close for several minutes before returning him to his bed.

Missie checked the coffeepot on her small stove. The full-sized stove she had brought from "home" at her mama's insistence remained packed in its crate. It was too big for the little sod house. Missie pushed the kettle toward the center so that the water would boil. Willie might soon be in and he would be chilled to the bone. But it was Henry's voice that Missie heard first, just outside the door.

"Still think thet we can't put it off any longer—no matter what else needs to be done. Snow could come anytime."

"Yeah," Willie agreed, "yer right. Shouldn't a' let it go this long. We'll plan on first thing in the mornin'. We'll use two wagons an' all the hands."

"Ya think they'll mind?"

"I'm boss, ain't I?"

"Sure ya are." Missie sensed a grin in Henry's voice. "But I reckon they might think thet they was hired on to punch cows—not pick up chips."

"We'll see," Willie said.

Oh, Missie thought, *if only it means what I hope it means.*

The next morning, soon after breakfast, two wagons and five

men set out to gather chips for the winter fires. All day long they shuttled back and forth. The cook's supply was heaped beside the cookshack, but Missie was favored. Her pile was stored in a sod shed just behind the house. This would save her the struggle of breaking frozen chips out of the snow.

Missie nearly cried with relief as she watched her shanty fill. Gathering chips would have been an increasingly difficult task with the coming of the winter snow. "Thank you, God," her heart whispered, "And thank you, Willie—an' all of you." Missie felt light with her thankfulness. She groped for a way to express her deep gratitude. At the same time she reached for her large coffee-pot and filled it to the brim. She'd at least have steaming coffee waiting to warm the men on their next trip in.

The next day the men also hauled, and even the next—piling the overflow beside the shed. To Missie it looked like the supply would last forever. It did to some of the hands also. But Willie declared that he wanted to be absolutely sure that his wife had plenty on hand for warm fires throughout the coming winter.

Missie's days became easier after the chips had been gathered. But her time was also more difficult to fill with activity. The little room needed very little attention. Missie swept *at* the floor, made up the bed, prepared the meals and washed the dishes. Of course, she often had to make a trip to the spring when she ran out of the water, which Willie had hauled before leaving for his daily duties. Beyond that, there wasn't much to fill her hours.

She decided to knit socks for Henry—then continued to knit a pair for each of the ranch hands. She would have them ready for Christmas. After the socks were finished and Missie's idle hands once again felt useless, she decided to make each of the men heavy woolen mittens for the winter days ahead. She hesitated—not sure if cowboys would scorn such things as woolen mittens, but she proceeded anyway.

Missie did not know the men well. The tall, lean, hard-faced one with the hook-nose was Clem. The shorter, tobacco-spitting one was Sandy.

Missie was a bit more familiar with Cookie—the cook. He was a quiet but pleasant man whose sharp eyes seemingly missed nothing. His face was plain until lit with a smile—which occurred whenever he saw Missie or her small son. Cookie walked with a bad limp—which explained why he was content to cook rather than ride the range with the other men. A bad fall while breaking a horse was his explanation for the faulty hip and leg. Missie was glad that he was around, for though they rarely conversed, his occasional nod and grin brightened her day a bit.

The baby's laundry was Missie's most trying task. The water had to be hauled from the spring below the house; though Willie filled the two available pails before he left in the morning, it wasn't nearly enough for Missie to do the job. The little stove was too small to hold a tub or a boiler, so Missie had to heat the water kettle by kettle. By the time she had the next kettleful hot, the first one had cooled. Having been schooled to wash clothes in *hot* water, she found her patience sorely tested.

The first winter storm attacked with fury. Driving wind whipped cutting sleet, smashing it against the small windows, swirling it round each corner of the sod house. The snow stacked in drifts and buried any obstacle in its pathway. Missie prayed that her little sod shack would be able to stand against the storm's anger.

Willie insisted on being *out* when Missie felt it was only sensible for him to be *in*. All hands rode throughout the day to insure that the three hundred cattle now wearing the Hanging W brand were not lost in the storm.

They returned late in the afternoon, having hazed the cattle into a boxed canyon which they hoped would offer some protection from the worst of the weather.

Still, Willie fretted and paced as he watched the driving snow.

The storm had lost some of its fury by the next afternoon, and Henry and Sandy rode out to check the stock. They reported back that all were accounted for. Willie relaxed again.

The snow did not melt away, and Missie realized that winter was not about to retreat. The spring soon froze over; Missie was forced to melt snow for their water supply. It was a tedious task, particularly on her washday. She didn't care for the taste of snow water, either, but gradually adjusted to it.

Missie's days were uneventful, repetitious. She was bored. The deep drifts all about the little sod house blocked her view of even the empty, frost-painted hills. The tasks of bringing her fuel for her fire and melting enough snow to keep water in the house provided Missie with nothing except *work*.

How glad Missie was for tiny Nathan. As he became aware of what was happening around him, and his smile greeted Missie when she looked over at him in his bed, her days took on some meaning and purpose. She talked to him constantly. Without him the dark walls of the tiny sod shanty would have been a prison for Missie during those long, empty, wintry days.

"Thank You, Father," Missie prayed often. "Thank You for our son."

Chapter 27

Christmas

One day, as Missie hung the baby's laundry from the lines strung in the one-room house, she suddenly realized to her surprise that only a few days remained until Christmas.

She ducked under a line of hanging diapers and made her way to another homemade calendar clipped on the wall. It was true. There were only four days 'til Christmas.

She looked about her. Christmas? Here? She blinked away tears and scolded herself. But the aching feeling within her was not to be shaken so easily. What could she possibly do to make this shanty ready for Christmas?

That evening as she and Willie sat at their small table to eat their stew and biscuits, Missie brought up the subject.

"Did you realize that in just four days it's Christmas?"

"Christmas?" Willie said, looking surprised. "Christmas already? Boy, how time does fly!"

Missie felt a sharp retort forming on her tongue, but she refused to voice it.

"Christmas!" Willie repeated. "I can hardly believe it."

He finished the biscuit that he was eating. "Guess I can't provide ya with a turkey. Will a roast of venison do?"

"I reckon."

"Be kinda hard havin' Christmas alone, won't it?"

"I've been thinkin' on that." Missie said. "Why don't we have the hands in?"

"In *here*?"

"Why not?"

Willie stared at the lines of hanging baby things. "Not much room."

"I know, but we could make do."

"They could come two at a time, I guess."

"That wouldn't be *Christmas*."

"How'll ya do it, then?"

"I'll set the food out on the table an' the stove an' we'll just help ourselves and sit wherever we fit—on the stools, on the bed—wherever. I think there's one more stool in the bunkhouse—an' Cookie has one in the cookhouse."

Willie laughed. "You've got yer heart set on it, ain't ya?"

Missie lowered her head but made no comment.

"Okay," said Willie, "invite the men."

"Would you invite them, please, Willie? I—I don't see them much."

"Sure, I'll invite 'em. Fer what time?"

"Let's make it one o'clock."

Willie nodded. "An' I'll git ya thet venison roast."

"Could Cookie do the roast in his stove? Then I can have mine free for the other things."

Willie nodded again. "I'll talk to 'im."

Cookie agreed to do the roast, and when the day arrived Missie went to work on the remainder of the meal. She didn't have much to work with but what she lacked in ingredients, she made up for with ingenuity. She had been hoarding some of her mother's preserves for just such a time as this. She opened them now and used some of the fruit to fill tart shells. She prepared some of the last canned carrots and beans from home to go with the roast venison. The only potatoes left were a few precious ones that she had kept, hoping to plant them in the spring. They looked sorry and neglected, but Missie still prayed that they might have the germ of life left in them. She refused to use any of them now, although the thought of potatoes with the meal made her mouth water. Instead, she baked a big batch of fluffy biscuits and set out her last jar of honey to go with them.

When the men arrived, Cookie proudly carrying his roast of venison, Missie was ready for them.

"Before we eat," Willie said, "I have something else to bring in. We don't have much room, iffen ya noticed"—this brought a guffaw from the men—"so I left it in the other shed."

He soon returned carrying a scrub bush, held upright in a small pail. On its tiny branches hung little bows made from Missie's scraps of yarn.

"Didn't rightly seem like Christmas without a tree," he said apologetically. The men whooped and Missie cried.

When the commotion had died down, Willie moved with difficulty to the middle of the room and led them in prayer:

"Father, we have much to thank You fer. Fer the good-smellin' food of which we are about to partake; fer the warmth of this little room in which we are to share it; fer friends who are here with us an' those who are far away; fer the memories of other Christmases spent with those we love; fer Nathan Isaiah, our healthy son; and most of all, God, fer my wife who has blessed us all by givin' us this Christmas. We are reminded thet all of these blessin's are extras. Yer special gift to us on this day was Yer Son. We accept thet Gift with our thanks. Amen."

As the menfolk devoured the tasty and plentiful food, Missie sat quietly. She tried to keep her thoughts from wandering to her parents' home. What would it be like if she could be there, right now? In a house big enough to serve a whole family in comfort, with fresh butter, mashed potatoes, turkey, baked squash, and apple pie topped with whipped cream.

She looked at her plate filled with sliced venison and gravy, canned carrots with no garnish, canned yellow beans, and a biscuit with no butter. However, many days during the last year, she had partaken of even simpler fare. She realized that she was eating a rather sumptuous feast, in comparison. The men obviously felt it was such; and when it came time for the tarts and coffee, they licked their lips in anticipation. Missie picked her way across the room to check on Nathan. One could barely move without tripping over feet but the close proximity just made it easier for laughing together.

"Son," she whispered to the baby, "you're not gonna remember one thing 'bout this, but I want you to get in on it anyway. Your very first Christmas, and I don't even have anything to give you—but a kiss, an' laughter of friends." She took him in her arms.

After the meal, Missie summoned all of her courage and presented each one of the men with a pair of socks and woolen mittens. She was unprepared for their deep appreciation. She realized that for some of them it may have been their first Christmas gift since they were small boys at home.

Cookie shifted his position to "git outta the smoke from the blasted fire—it's a makin' my eyes water."

Clem swallowed over and over, his Adam's apple lurching up and down.

Missie prayed that none of them would feel embarrassed at having nothing to give in return.

After the men had expressed their thanks as best as they could, Missie began timidly, "Now I want to say thank you for your gift to me."

Five pairs of eyes—six, counting Nathan's—swung to her face. There she sat, just a little scrap of a girl-woman, youthful and pretty, her cheeks glowing with health, her eyes sparkling near tears, her trim figure clothed attractively in a bright calico, the tiny, fair-skinned, chubby-cheeked Nathan contentedly in her arms studying her face.

"I want to thank you," she said shyly, "for workin' so faithfully for my husband, for makin' his load—an' thus mine—easier, for not demandin' things that we can't provide." She hesitated, then smiled, "But most of all, I want to thank you for the good supply of chips that you didn't fuss 'bout haulin'. I've been thankful over an' over for those chips."

Missie couldn't suppress a giggle. Though the men realized

that she was sincere in her thankfulness, they also saw the humor in it and gladly laughed with her.

Though unaware of it at that moment, Missie had just made some friends for life. Not one of those men sitting round her tiny shanty would have denied her anything that was in their power to provide.

Later, Henry brought in his guitar and they sang together. Cookie just sat and listened. Sandy whistled a few lines now and then. But Clem, to Missie's surprise, seemed to know by heart most of the traditional carols.

It was hard to break up the little gathering. Several times Missie added more chips to her fire. Little Nathan made the rounds from one pair of arms to another. Even the tough-looking Clem took a turn holding the baby.

At last Missie put the coffeepot back on and boiled a fresh pot. She was glad that she had made enough tarts for each of them to have another one with their coffee.

The men lingered over their tarts and coffee but finally took their leave, tramping their way through the snow back to the bunkhouse.

Missie hummed softly as she washed the dishes—there had been no point trying to find room to wash them earlier. Willie put on his hat and coat and left for the barn, Missie assumed, to check the horses.

Missie had finished the dishes and was feeding Nathan when Willie returned bearing a box. Missie looked astonished, and he answered her unasked question.

"I did my Christmas shopping 'fore we left Tettsford." He set his box on the table and began to unpack it.

" 'Fraid my gift don't seem too fittin' like in these surroundin's. I was sorta seein' it in our *real* house when I bought it, I guess. Anyway, I thought thet I'd show it to ya, an' then we can sorta pack it off again." Willie lifted from the box the most beautiful fruit bowl that Missie had ever seen.

She gasped, "Willie! It's beautiful."

Willie was relieved when he saw that the bowl had brought her pleasure. He set it gently on the table.

"I'll let ya git a better look at it when yer done with Nathan.

Then I'll pack it on back—out of yer way."

"Oh, no," Missie protested. "Just leave it."

She laid the baby on the bed and went to the table to pick up the bowl.

"It's lovely," she said, her fingers caressing it. "Thank you, Willie."

She reached up to kiss him. "An' I don't want you to pack it away—please. It'll be a reminder—an' a promise. I—I need it here. Don't you see?"

Willie held her close. "I see."

After a moment of silence, Willie spoke softly.

"Missie, I wonder—I wonder iffen you'll ever know jest how happy ya made five people today?"

"Five?"

"Those four cowpokes—an' *me*."

Missie's eyes gleamed.

"Then make it *six*, Willie—'cause in doin' what I could, the pleasure all poured right back on me. An' I got the biggest helpin' of happiness myself!"

Chapter 28

Setbacks

After the anticipation and preparation for Christmas, the winter days fell back into their previous monotony. At times Missie felt that she could endure no more, confined as she was in her stuffy sod shanty. Her only company for most of her days was baby Nathan. She feared that she might spoil him with all the attention he received. It was a good thing that he fussed very little, for Missie used every little cry or complaint as an excuse to pamper and cuddle him. He responded with toothless smiles and waving fists.

When he slept, Missie tried to find other things to keep herself busy. Her hands had long since run out of materials for crafts and activities to occupy them, and the walls of the room seemed to press ever more closely about her. She no longer made daily treks to the fuel shack; ever since Christmas, a good supply of chips appeared beside her door every day before she crawled out of bed. Missie never discovered which one of the men delivered them.

Baby Nathan gained weight, gurgled and cooed, and tried to

chew everything that his small hands could get to his mouth. Soon it became difficult to find a safe place to leave the wee child.

Though time with him was somewhat limited, Willie also doted on his son. Missie sometimes teased that if it had not been for Nathan, Willie would have been content to live out with his precious cows! When Nathan began to squeal at the sight of his daddy and laugh at his roughhouse play, Willie found it even harder to leave the house and go back to the stock.

Missie was having glimmers of hope that winter was almost over when a sudden, angry-sounding wind swept in from the north. It caught them off guard, and before the men could even saddle up to go look after the cows, the snow came—the swishing, blinding clouds of it seemed set on devouring everything in its path. Willie realized that it was foolhardy to send men out in such a storm. He would just have to leave the animals on their own and hope that they could find some shelter.

The storm moved on after two days. By then the drifts of snow had piled high all around. The shanty's door was almost buried by the whiteness. Willie had to wait for the ranch hands to dig him out.

When they were finally able to leave their quarters, the men quickly saddled up to go out looking for the range cattle in the hills. After combing the hills for three days, the reports were heartbreaking. At least seventy-five head of cattle had been lost in the storm. Missie cried. Willie tried to assure her that they'd make out fine, that temporary setbacks were to be expected; but Missie could see a troubled look in his own eyes. They both turned again to their Isaiah passage for comfort and strength.

In February one of the milk cows calved, and Missie felt like she had been handed an incomparable treasure. Even the loss of the cattle the week before was put from her mind. What marvelous possibilities for sparking up their diet, with milk on hand!

"What I couldn't do now, if I just had some eggs," she said. She promised herself that as soon as possible she'd do something about that.

Spring eventually did come—slowly, almost unnoticeably,

until one day Missie realized that there was a feeling of faint warmth in the air. The drifts of snow began to shrink and gradually dark spots of earth appeared. The spring started to trickle again and the stubby bushes beside it began to dress in a shy green.

Missie ached for the sight of budding trees, of blossoming shrubs, but only empty hills, stretched away from her gaze. To her great joy, a few flowers timidly made their appearance; Missie couldn't resist picking some to grace her table. In the gloom of the little sod house, one had to bend over the tin cup that held the flowers, in order to fully appreciate the tiny scraps of color.

As the snow receded, the men spent much more time out on the range, watching the cattle vigilantly. Spring calves were arriving daily; they would not totter about many days before the "Hanging W," Willie's brand, would show on their flanks.

Missie did not care for the name attached to Willie's ranch, not in favor of "hanging" even a *W*. But Willie laughed at her squeamishness. All of Willie's stock bore the brand.

The hard range riding of spring roundup had begun. Day after day the men rode and gathered the scattered stock and their calves. They were all driven to the wide box-canyon where they had been protected during the first winter storm. When the roundup was completed, the men counted one hundred ninety-eight head of cattle and one hundred and six calves.

"Even so," Willie maintained, "thet's a few more than we started with."

The wagons were moved out to the canyon to serve as bunkhouses during the spring branding. Cookie slept in the chow wagon, as well as using it for kitchen, supply shack and blacksmith shop.

The men were divided into shifts for the night hours, and Willie and Sandy took the first hours.

It wasn't long until the cattle adjusted to their more confined surroundings. The lowing and milling subsided and they bedded down for the night.

After midnight, Henry and Clem took over the night-watch duties. Sandy and Willie gladly unsaddled their mounts and cozied up to Cookie's open fire. They drank mugs of hot coffee to warm their bones before trying to get a few hours of sleep. The early morning sun would soon summon them to another busy day with the branding irons.

Shortly before daybreak, mayhem broke loose. At first Henry and Clem were unable to pinpoint the source of the sudden restlessless and shifting of the herd. By the time they realized the cause, they found themselves helpless.

A band of rustlers was driving off a large portion of the herd. Henry and Clem rode hard, but in spite of their best efforts they were able to cut back only the stragglers from the stampeding cattle. No shots had been fired, but Henry and Clem had counted, in spite of the darkness and confusion, at least five rustlers. By the time the sleeping men in the wagons heard the commotion and recognized what it was, it was too late for them to assist.

The next morning the discouraged men ranged out farther, gathering the few head that had somehow eluded the rustlers. After all the cattle in their possession had been gathered and counted, Willie found that his herd now numbered only fifty-four head of full-grown cattle and thirty-two calves.

After the final count, Willie turned away, his shoulders slumped in defeat. He had known all along that he would suffer some losses to rustlers, but he had dared to hope that the numbers would be few and over a longer period of time. *Why!* he asked himself, *Why did I think that we would be spared when so many other ranchers have been completely wiped out? I should feel lucky to have any cattle left, any at all.*

Willie swallowed the hard lump in his throat, and lifted his broad-brimmed hat to wipe the dust from his brow. The sick feeling in the pit of his stomach refused to leave. Could he get back on his feet? How long would it take? If he had been more patient and had worked for another year before coming out to his ranch, he could have laid aside enough cash to cover such a tragedy.

Now the only extra cash he had was the money for Missie's house. How could he ever tell her? Even now he could picture those frank, blue eyes, intense with hurt and fright from the news.

Though he wished with every ounce of his being that he could do so, he knew it would be useless and untruthful to try to keep it from her. She deserved to know the truth—even to know the seriousness of their situation. But Willie determined that in every way possible he would try to shield her from the pain and the fear that came with the knowing.

Willie presented Missie with the facts as honestly and simply as he knew how. He talked like it was an inevitable event—the loss of his cattle; but deep down, Missie knew better. She ached for him. If only there was some way that she could help him.

Then within her breast arose a tiny surge of hope. Maybe now he would be satisfied to have tried his dream and be content to go back home. But Willie had no such intention. Instead, to Missie's surprise, he told his men that as soon as the work could be started, they would begin building the permanent ranch house.

Missie said nothing until they were alone that night. She began very carefully, "I overheard you discussin' with the hands your plans for buildin'."

"Yeah, iffen it's gonna be ready as planned we need to git started."

"But, Willie," Missie protested softly. "Can we afford it?"

"What ya meanin'?"

"Well, with the cattle losses an' all."

"Thet changes nothin'. The money for the house has been set aside."

"But what 'bout rebuildin' the herd?"

"Thet'll jest have to wait."

"But can it? I mean, if we don't have a herd, there won't be cattle to sell, an' if—"

"There'll be some—eventually. An' I promised ya a house. We can't do both, Missie; an' the house comes first."

"Willie, listen." Missie felt afraid that she might later regret what she was about to say. But she had to say it: "Willie, I know 'bout your promise. I know that you want to keep it—an' you will. But it could be postponed, Willie, for just a bit—until—until we have the cattle to sell. If we stay in this house, just for now, and use the put-aside money to help rebuild the herd, then next year—well, we could build our house then."

Missie saw Willie's jaw muscles tighten as if he was fighting for control.

"Please, Willie," she coaxed. "The cattle are important to *me* too, you know."

"But ya couldn't keep on livin' here, not fer another whole year—another winter."

" 'Course I could," she hurried on with as much conviction as she could muster. "I'm gettin' used to it now. It's not very big, but it's warm. And now that spring is here, Nathan an' I can go outside more. We'll manage. Honest!"

Silence followed. For a time Missie wondered if she had been refused. She didn't know whether to feel relieved or sorry. The house was small and difficult. Yet she knew that if Willie was intending to stay, and it seemed that indeed he was, then he needed to rebuild that herd. Without it their future was very insecure. Her love for Willie drove her to decide for his happiness. He'd never be happy to admit defeat, to leave his beloved hills and valleys and return back East.

Oh, God, she prayed silently, *help me to support Willie in spite of what I want. Keep Your promise to uphold me now.* And He did.

Missie felt peace go through her being. The next thing she knew, Willie was pulling her close. She understood that Willie was accepting her gift of postponement on the house in order to rebuild his herd. She reached her hand up to touch his cheeks and felt the dampness. Willie was crying.

Chapter 29

Missie's Garden

With the smell of spring in the air, Missie was even more rest-less as she anxiously waited for the final disappearance of snow. Nathan, more active now, needed room in which to explore. Missie dared not leave him in the small sod house longer than a dash out back for more chips or to scoop up a pail of snow for her water supply.

She had tired of the snow water, but she did not feel that it was any longer safe for her to go to the trickling spring and leave the baby alone in the house; she could not carry him and a buck-et of water too. But her reason did not keep her from *wanting* to go to the spring. Just the sight of running water would be a sign to her that spring was truly here.

She needed desperately an escape from the four tight walls. She also needed a change of activity. Her fingers felt heavy and numb from the hours of knitting and sewing. She was just plain bored—bored with everything about her world.

Missie looked out on the sparkling day and, as many times in the past, wished with all her heart that she had some excuse to be out in the sunshine. If only she could saddle a horse and go out onto the prairies like the menfolk did. But with no one to leave small Nathan with, the idea was not workable.

Or was it?

Missie suddenly recalled a nostalgic item that she had slipped into one of the boxes when packing. She had found it tucked in the back of a drawer at home and, with tear-filled eyes, she had smuggled it in among some blankets. To another's eyes it would have simply been some kind of strange contraption, but to Missie it was *love* wrapped up in one simple, practical piece of equipment. Though Missie had no recollection of being carried in the backpack, her mama had long ago showed it to her and explained how her pa had lovingly fashioned it in order to carry her with him after she, just a tiny girl, had lost her first mother; he never left her at home alone while he plowed his fields and did his choring. Missie ran to the storage shed in her eagerness. With the backpack she would be able to take that horseback ride, and the baby would be able to join her!

Once the backpack had been located and shown to Willie, he selected a gentle mare and made her available to Missie whenever she wished to ride. Now some of the boredom would be gone from Missie's days. But even with the backpack, she could not go far before Baby Nathan became heavy to carry and Missie would be forced to return to the little shanty.

Missie was also bored with the sameness of the food that she had to prepare every day. Nothing tasted good anymore—nothing was fresh. Canned, dried and bland—described everything she had to prepare. No amount of herbs and spices seemed to improve it any. She wondered if Willie found it as unpalatable as she did. But, of course, Willie was too much of a gentleman to say so.

It seemed to Missie's worn, restless spirit that planting a garden would revive her again—and so she paced back and forth, willing the snow to go away. When fresh flurries sent scattered flakes whirling through the still crisp air, Missie wiped tears of disappointment on her apron.

Finally the snow flurries changed to rain showers, and Missie's hopes grew.

The snow melted reluctantly—especially where it had drifted by the spring—the very place Missie wanted for her garden. She felt sorely tempted to go out with a shovel, but checked herself from such foolishness. The snow gradually lost the battle, and one day when Missie went to check she was surprised and thrilled to find all traces of the winter's cold and ice gone. She began hinting to Willie that he put a plow to the sod. Willie showed more patience than Missie.

"Be a bit early yet," he insisted. "The ground hasn't had a fair chance to warm. An' remember, this ain't the East. We're right close to the mountains here, an' frosts still come on the early spring nights."

But Missie could not bear the thought of being detained. Willie, realizing what it meant to her, relented and plowed the spot, though he was sure that it was far too early to do so.

Missie felt released from captivity as she sorted her seeds and set off for planting. She took a blanket on which to deposit Nathan, and set to work. She was sure that the baby would be as joyful as she, at finally being free from the four walls of the shanty, but he looked about in a perplexed manner and began to fuss. Missie tried to amuse him, but he continued to wail. She then turned him over onto his tummy and patted him gently until he fell asleep. At least the fresh air would do him good.

"You're missin' so much by sleeping, my boy," she whispered. "The clear blue sky, the feel of the spring air, the smell of the soil. I do hope that someday you appreciate it all. But for now, your mama will just enjoy it for you."

Missie went to her planting. She was so glad that she had plenty of seed. She was so hungry for green, growing things; and her impatience mounted with each seed that she dropped into the ground. She could almost smell the vegetables cooking in the days ahead. The imagined taste and tang of them was pungent even in her thoughts.

Her job ended too soon; the little garden was planted. Nathan still slept, so Missie sat down beside him on the blanket and listened to the soft gurgle of the spring only a few paces away. It was so good to feel alive again. She thanked God that life was not always winter, that spring always came at last—to chase away the cold and heaviness, and to release one to warmth and movement again.

Nathan awoke and Missie reached for him. She talked to him, begging him to behold and enjoy what she saw, to feel the things that she felt, to breathe as deeply as she breathed. But all that the baby seemed in need of, or atune to, was the face and arms of the mother who held him close and cooed words of love to him. At length Missie gathered everything together, bundled up her baby and headed back to her sod house. Nathan was hungry, she knew, and would soon be demanding his dinner.

That very night it snowed. When Missie looked out the next morning, hoping to see another fair and sunny day, she saw instead a thin layer of white over the entire world. Willie saw her face and heard her sharp gasp. He joined her at the window, ducking his head so that he could look out.

"Moisture!" he said quickly. "Be mighty good fer those seeds of yers. Soon's the sun's up to work on it, it'll soak in real good."

Missie changed her mind about crying and gave Willie a rueful smile instead. She didn't know if Willie was right, but she wanted him to know that she loved him for his concern for her.

The sun did melt the snow, almost as soon as its warm fingers began to reach out over the brown earth, sending up to heaven little shimmering mists, like dancing vapors.

There were other mornings when Missie awoke to scattering snowfalls or frost on the ground. On such mornings she prayed that none of her brave little plants had as yet lifted their heads from the protective soil bed. Though Missie knew that her seedlings were safe as long as they were not exposed, yet she longed for their appearance. Daily she watched for signs of life in her garden. Eventually it came—a green blade here and there; a suggestion of a green spray down a row; a pair of tiny leaves breaking forth, gradually joined by others until a row could be defined. At length Missie was able to recognize onions, radishes, beans, peas and carrots. Her garden was growing.

And then one night—the dreaded frost came. Some of the hardier vegetables were seemingly untouched, but the more tender things wilted and curled up tightly against the ground.

"Still plenty of time fer replantin'," Willie assured. "Ya want me to turn those rows with the spade?"

Missie shook her head.

"The exercise will be good for me—an' I know how busy you are."

She replanted, and again watched for new growth. It came—but it seemed, oh, so slow this time.

One day as Missie checked on her garden, she was surprised to find an onion that made a fair-sized bite. It wasn't big, really, but when she pulled it up, it truly did smell like an onion. She pulled off its outer skin and popped it into her mouth. Oh, it tasted good! She had almost forgotten how good a green onion tasted. She reached for another and devoured it, too. Down the row she went, searching, pulling, and eating, until at length she turned and looked at the trail of discarded tops that she had left behind. She was shocked at how many she had eaten. As she bent to pick up the top nearest to her, she felt the results of a lunch of onions. Missie burped—then giggled. "Oh, my," she said. "If Willie could see what a pig I've been!"

Guiltily Missie retraced her steps, picking up onion tops so that her gluttony would not be so obvious. She pulled a few more onions to season a stew, then, gathering Nathan up, returned to the house.

The onions did not sit well, and Missie felt an uneasiness in her stomach for the remainder of the day. By the time Willie came for his supper she wished that she didn't have to join him at the table. Even the savory smell of the onions in the stew could not tempt her. Willie observed her white face and was instantly concerned.

"Ya sick?"

"Just off my feed a little."

"Yer sure?"

"Yeah—I'm sure."

"Ya'd best lie down—I'll look after myself. Where's the problem? Ya got a pain somewhere?"

"Just a little."

"Where?"

"My stomach's a mite upset."

"Taken any of yer ma's medicine? There's stuff there fer—"

"It'll pass."

Willie looked unconvinced. Missie was beginning to *feel* unconvinced as well. She lay down on the bed, almost groaning as she did so. Willie went to cover her. Then lifted the box of medical supplies onto the table, sorting through bottles and tins, carefully reading each label.

"Describe what yer feelin'," he said, "an' I'll know better what to look fer."

Missie answered with a loud belch and then a giggle. Willie wheeled around, wondering if the loneliness of the western prairies had finally gotten to her, or if she had somehow gotten into some of Cookie's "pain-killer." Missie was actually laughing—not hysterical laughter, but controlled mirth, and there was a twinkle in her eye.

"I doubt if you'll be findin' anything to counteract onions," she said.

"Onions?"

"*My* onions. They're big enough to eat—an' I just went right at 'em an' made a pig of myself," she grinned weakly. "Oh, Willie, they tasted so good—at first. But," she added seriously, "they're gettin' so they don't taste near so good now."

"Ya mean—ya ate onions until. . . ?" Willie said incredulously, not even finishing his question.

Missie nodded—and burped again.

The concern was gone from Willie's face; he lowered himself onto a stool and howled. "Ya little goose," he finally said when he could speak, and they laughed together. He came over to her bed, reached down to kiss her, then backed away.

"Ma'am, you *did* eat onions," he said wrinkling his nose.

"Put away yer medicines, I'll be fine in the mornin'."

Willie still insisted that she take something for indigestion, then tucked Missie in so that she could sleep.

Missie *was* fine again the next morning—but Baby Nathan was not. He fussed and fretted all day. Missie scolded herself over and over for not considering him before she attacked the onion patch. But when Missie's stomach had remedied itself and Baby Nathan again slept quietly, Missie smiled to herself. Every mouthful of the fresh, crisp onions had been worth it. They had tasted *that good.*

Chapter 30

Summer

Summer had arrived at last. Missie's garden was daily supplying their table with a variety of tasty, fresh produce. Willie had purchased cattle to bolster his herd, and had decided that what he must do next was to hire more riders before the cattle were brought to the Hanging W. This would insure proper protection day and night, once they were wearing his brand. He and Henry spent a number of days constructing another sod bunkhouse so that the men to be hired would have a place to bed down. After the new building was completed, Willie prepared for a trip to town, to pick up the necessary supplies and also scout out the new ranch hands. He and Henry would each drive a wagon. They left on a Thursday.

Missie looked at her homemade calendar and allowed them three weeks for the trip. Oh, how she wished that she could have gone too. She longed so much for a chat with a woman, for a browse through a shop, for tea and cake. But she knew that the trip would be long and the weather hot, so she had forced herself to keep from asking Willie for permission to go.

She wrote notes to Melinda, Kathy and the preacher and his wife. She then wrote a longer letter to Mrs. Taylorson, bringing her up-to-date on all the things that Nathan could now do, or was attempting to do.

She and Willie worked carefully on the supply list. Missie tried to think of all of the things that she might need over the next year.

It was difficult for Missie to think of everything that her growing baby would need. Nathan had grown and changed so much already that it was hard to keep up with him even day by day. How could she possibly know what Nathan would need in a year's time? He would be walking and playing outside—needing shoes and shirts and pants. How did one shop for the needs of a fast-growing son? Missie decided that Willie would need some help. She composed a separate list that Willie was to give to Melinda. It was for yarns, sewing fabrics, and two special gifts for Willie—one for his fast-approaching birthday and one for Christmas. She also asked Melinda to choose a small toy for Nathan's first birthday.

Willie tucked away Missie's list for Melinda, then checked and rechecked their supply list. He finally turned to Missie.

"Is there anythin' *special* thet ya be wantin'?"

Missie did not hesitate. "Some chickens," she said. " 'Bout a dozen hens an' a couple of roosters."

Willie's mouth dropped open. "Chickens?"

"Yeah, chickens. Do you realize what it would mean to have chickens? We could have eggs—fried, boiled an' scrambled—and roast chicken, fried chicken, chicken an' dumplin's—"

"Whoa," Willie said. "I'm not doubtin' none the merits of chickens—but *here*?"

"And why not?"

"We don't have the feed."

"They can scrounge for themselves."

"They'd starve!"

"Then we'll just have to buy feed."

"An' they'd need a henhouse."

"They could live in a sod hut just as well as I can," said Missie stubbornly.

Willie saw that her mind was made up.

"Okay," he laughed. "I'll see what I can do 'bout chickens—but I won't make any promises."

"That's all I'm askin'," Missie said, satisfied that Willie would indeed try.

Chapter 31

Maria

If Missie had been bored and lonely before, she was doubly so now with Willie gone. Each day she took Nathan out for a short walk or horseback ride. She did not dare go far and could only go out in the morning before the sun got too hot. While Nathan slept, she often went to the spring or to her garden. She was pleased that her garden was doing well. Each time that she went down there she took the time to pull some weeds and pour water on her thirsty plants.

She stopped to chat briefly with Cookie once in a while. He seemed to feel responsible for her with Willie gone. Missie was touched by his trips to the spring on her behalf, hobbling along with her buckets of water.

She was careful to be inside her small hut during the heat of the day and was often surprised that the cozy little shanty of the winter was also cool in the summer. It got stuffy though, and Missie often yearned for a fresh, cooling breath of summer air, such as she had enjoyed beneath the tall shade trees back home.

The days managed to crawl by, one by one. Soon Missie was

down to day eighteen. Her eyes kept searching the distant hills. She hoped that by some miracle Willie would complete his tasks in less time than anticipated and be home early.

One afternoon as Missie's eyes again swept over the hills visible through her window, she was surprised to see a lone rider heading directly toward the house.

Who could that be? she puzzled. *It's sure not Clem or Sandy.* As the rider neared the house, Missie let out a gasp of unbelief.

"It's a woman!" she exclaimed aloud, bursting through the door and waking small Nathan with her sharp cry and rush of activity.

Tears ran down Missie's cheeks as she ran toward the rider. She hadn't realized just how starved she was for the company of a woman. Oh, to talk, to laugh, to visit, to sip tea—oh, the joy of it.

Missie brushed at her cheeks and forced herself to a walk as the woman dismounted—the visitor might be frightened away thinking she was demented. They stood and gazed at one another, a smile spreading over their faces. Missie wondered if she detected loneliness in the woman's eyes.

Missie's visitor was hardly more than a girl, with dusky skin, long, loose-flowing dark hair, and black eyes. Her full lips suggested that they liked to laugh. Missie felt drawn to her new friend immediately.

"Oh," she cried, "I'm so glad to see you." She rushed forward and threw her arms around the girl, laughing and crying at the same time. The stranger responded and Missie received a warm hug in return.

They stepped back and studied one another.

"Where did you come from?" Missie asked. To her amazement the girl answered with words that she could not comprehend.

Missie frowned.

"I'm sorry," she said, "I don't understand you. You'll have to speak English."

A smooth flow of words followed, but again they meant nothing to Missie.

"You mean, you don't speak English?"

The girl just shrugged. Missie wanted to cry, but checked herself and took the girl's arm.

"Well, come in anyway," she said. "At least we can have some tea."

She led the young woman to her tiny sod house and pointed to a stool. She then began to build a fire in her little stove for tea. Upon hearing an exclamation of joy, Missie turned to see the girl bending over Nathan. He had gotten over his fright with Missie's startled exclamation and was lying on the bed playing with his fingers. She looked back at Missie and spoke. From the look in her eyes, Missie took the question to be concerning Nathan and she nodded her head in approval.

The young woman gathered the baby to her, her face full of pleasure. She crooned to the baby and spoke softly. Nathan could not have understood the words but he grasped the meaning. He smiled and cooed in return.

The fire caught quickly, and Missie pushed the kettle to the center, then joined the girl.

"Nathan," she said, indicating the baby.

"Na-tan," the girl repeated.

Missie pointed to herself.

"Missie," she said.

"Mis-see." The girl smiled, then added, "Maria," pointing to herself.

"Maria."

There was so much that Missie wanted to talk about, so much that she wanted to ask. But all they could do was play with Nathan, smile at one another and sip tea.

At last Maria indicated that she must go. Missie could hardly bear the thought of losing her. She had needed her so much—the friendship of another woman. It made her think of her home, of her mother; and the thoughts of her mama made her think of all the precious times that they had shared together.

"Wait," she said, "before you go, would it be all right for us to—to pray together?"

Maria shrugged, not comprehending.

"Pray," Missie said, pointing to herself and to Maria and then folding her hands for prayer.

"Sí," said Maria, her face lighting up. "Sí." She knelt down beside her stool on the hard-packed earth of the shanty floor. Missie too knelt down.

"Dear God," Missie began, "thank You so much for sending Maria to me. Thank You that even though I can't talk to her, I can feel a friendship and warmth. May she be able to come again—soon, and may I be able to learn some of her words so that I can tell her how glad I am to have her. Thank You that we can pray together, and bless her now as she goes home—wherever home is for her. Amen."

Missie prepared to rise, but Maria's soft voice stopped her. Missie opened her eyes and saw her new friend with face upturned in prayer. Her folded hands grasped the beads that hung from her neck.

Maria's voice rose and fell, much like the gentle brook waters of the creek that ran by Missie's old home. Missie caught "Missee" and "Na-tan" in the flow of words and also recognized the "Amen."

They rose together and smiled at one another. Missie's cheeks were wet. She had never shared prayer with someone of another faith before. She only knew that this young woman, Maria, seemed to know Missie's God, and that by sharing these moments together in prayer, their spirits were uplifted and refreshed. Surely God himself had sent Maria. Missie stepped forward and gave her another warm embrace.

Chapter 32

Willie's Return

Missie had struck off the twenty-first day of Willie's trip, on her calendar, but still he had not come. There was no sight of dust or wagon on the northern hills, no sound of grinding wagon wheels. She kept his supper hot on the back of the stove, but the fresh biscuits cooled in spite of her efforts. She lit the lamp and tried to read. Her thoughts returned to the verse that she had for so many months been clinging to; she turned in the Bible to read it again. She would not have needed to look it up—she knew it by heart. But right then she needed the assurance of the printed page. "Fear thou not; for I am with thee: be not dismayed; for I am thy God; I will strengthen thee; yea, I will help thee; yea, I will uphold thee with the right hand of my righteousness."

Missie read the verse several times. Eventually she felt quieted enough to blow out the lamp and go to bed.

Again the next day, she searched the distant hills for small dots that might mean riders, or small clouds that could mean dust from churning wheels and tramping hoofs—but only the angry glare of the sun met her tired eyes. Dusk came and she was forced to give up her vigil. Again that night she read by lamp-light. Again she embraced the words of Isaiah 41:10. At length she crawled into bed by her small son, softly repeating the words to herself in an effort to drive the uneasiness from her heart.

The third day dawned and Missie again paced back and forth, scanning the hills for anything that moved. She prepared a third supper for an absent husband and tried to silence the uneasiness within her. What if Willie didn't come back? Her thoughts went to her mother and the ordeal that she had faced when her Clem did not return.

Who was she, Missie, to think that such a thing could not happen to her? Her heart seemed to flutter and then stand still, flutter again and remain silent. Missie threw herself on the bed.

"Oh, God," she cried, "I know that I've been readin' an' clingin' to Your Word, but I guess I haven't been believin' it, God—not really, not down deep in my heart. Help me, Lord. Help me to believe it, to really believe it, that no matter—no matter what happens, it's in Your hands and for my *good*. God, I turn it all over to You—my life—my Willie—everything, God. Help me to trust You with all that is mine."

Missie continued to sob softly until a deep sense of peace stole into her heart and gently stilled its wild beating.

She awakened much later to the thumping of hooves in the yard. She pulled herself up quickly and rushed to the window, expecting to see Willie's wagons. Instead, it was strange horsemen milling about in the bright moonlight. Cookie was approaching them.

"It's happened," Missie whispered. "Something's happened to Willie." Her weak knees buckled beneath her and she sank onto a stool. "O God, help me now—help me to trust You."

She laid her head on her arms on the table and steeled herself for the news that Cookie would bring. No tears came—only a dull, empty feeling.

It was Cookie's footsteps at her door. He called softly and she bid him enter. He stepped inside, with the moonlight washing over him. Missie knew that he could not see her where she sat in the darkness.

"Mrs. LaHaye?"

"Yes."

"Jest thought thet ya might hear an' wonder 'bout all the ruckus in the yard. The new hands thet yer husband hired have jest arrived. The wagons will be in tomorra."

Missie's pounding heart caught in her throat. The new hands! The wagons were a short distance behind them! Willie would be home tomorrow!

It took a moment for it all to sink in. She wanted to shout. She wanted to laugh. She wanted to just throw herself on her bed and cry in pure thankfulness. Instead she said in a choked voice, "Thank you, Cookie. I *was* wonderin'."

When the door was closed and Cookie was gone, she put her head back down on her arms and sobbed out her pent-up feelings in great bursts of joy. "Thank You, God, thank You. Oh, thank You."

Missie never told Willie of her anxious days of waiting or of her traumatic nighttime experience. She was sure that he could not possibly understand. When the wagons had pulled into the yard in the heat and the dust the following day, a calm and smiling Missie greeted her man. He had brought supplies, letters, news that could hardly keep—and he even brought her chickens.

Willie turned from Missie to give orders to the ranch hands, then followed her into their small house.

He held her close. "Oh, I've missed ya. I thought thet trail would *never* end. It jest seemed forever." He kissed her. "Did ya miss me—a little bit?" he teased.

"A little bit," Missie said, smiling to herself. "Yeah, a *little* bit."

Willie produced the letters, but even before Missie could read them, Willie had to give some news.

The preacher's wife had fallen and was laid up with a broken hip. Missie's heart went out to the poor woman.

Kathy Weiss had found herself a young man.

"Poor Henry!" cried Missie.

Willie smiled. "Poor Henry, nothin'. Do ya know, thet young rascal had us all fooled? He wasn't ever after Kathy—not a'tall. It was Melinda Emory, the young widow, right from the start.

Only Henry had to wait fer a proper time before lettin' her know his feelin's."

"Yer joshin'!" Missie spoke incredulously. "Melinda? Well, I'll be!"

"And," Willie went on, "Henry has gone so far as to get some land of his own right next to ours—and in a short while, we will have neighbors."

Missie could hardly contain herself. Melinda for a neighbor! What a joy that would be. Another woman she could see often, and enjoy her company. She could scarcely wait.

But Willie also had some other big news. "And guess what? They're gonna build a railroad. An' they have it figured to put the main cattle shippin' station jest eighteen or twenty miles southwest of us—maybe even a little closer—who knows fer sure? Ya know what thet means? A railroad, a town, people movin' in, connection with the East—before we know it, we'll have so many neighbors we'll be trippin' over each other."

Missie exclaimed, "Oh—oh," over and over, while the tears trickled down her face in amazement and happiness. "Willie, when? When?"

Willie spoke calmly. "Well, I'm sure it won't be tomorra-like. But they're workin' on the railroad fer sure—from the other end. It should git here within a couple years, fer sure—maybe even next year, some say. An' as soon as the line is in, the people will follow for certain. Always happens thet way. Jest think! A railroad an' shipping station. What thet will mean to the ranchers! No more long cattle drives with heavy losses. Every beef thet gits safely to market means a lot of dollars in a cattleman's pocket.

"We've come at jest the right time, Missie. Things have never looked better. From now on, every available acre of land will be snapped up at a big price, an' the price of cattle is bound to go up, too." Willie picked Missie up and attempted to swing her around in their small cramped quarters. He bumped into the table and bed.

"Silly small shack," he said. "We're gonna git us thet house just as soon as we sell some of thet herd next spring. Place ain't fit to live in."

"Oh, Willie," Missie chided—though secretly and silently she agreed with Willie's statement—"it's a home. We can eat, sleep an' keep dry here. That's not bad for starters."

Willie laughed as he hugged her.

"How's the boy?"

"He's been good."

"No more onions?"

"Only little snatches."

Willie gazed at his sleeping son.

"Look at 'im," he said softly. "He's gone an' growed by inches."

Willie couldn't resist; he gently lifted the baby into his arms. Nathan awoke. Surprise, then joy, made him squirm and wave his arms at the sight of his father.

Willie cuddled him close and kissed the soft head of hair. Missie blinked away happy tears.

"Got somethin' fer ya, Boy," Willie said to his son. "An' it weren't near the trouble of yer mama's confounded chickens."

"My chickens!" Missie squealed. "Where are they?"

"Well, I hope by now the boys have 'em corralled inside thet wire fence. What a squawkin', complainin' lot!"

"How many?"

"Couple roosters an' eleven hens—an' I had me one awful time to gather up thet many. Folks out here seem to know better than to bother with chickens."

Missie accepted the teasing and hurried out to see her flock. Willie followed behind her with the still-sleepy Nathan.

The men had just finished tacking up the wire mesh to poles that they had pounded into the ground. As Henry finished hanging the gate that he had quickly built for the enclosure, the other two men turned and left; let someone else do the fussing with the chickens; they had done more than their share in building the pen.

Willie passed Nathan to Missie and went to lift down the large crate. The chickens squawked and flapped as they were released, not appearing the least bit grateful to be set free. They were a sorry-looking lot, not at all like Marty's proud-strutting chickens back home. Missie wondered if she would ever be able to coax them to produce any eggs for her family. One of the hens did not leave the crate. She had succumbed to the heat of the trail or the lice that inflicted her, or perhaps some other malady. Willie said he would bury it later so it wouldn't draw any unwanted flies.

"Seems to me," he observed, "another good dose of louse powder might not hurt 'em any. I think we'll jest leave them outside—shut them out of their coop until I treat 'em again. I gave 'em all one good dustin' before I loaded 'em. Left a trail of dead lice from Tettsford Junction to home."

Missie laughed, but agreed. They did look like they could stand another good treatment of *something*.

"I'll do the dusting," Willie said, "but from then on, they're all yers. Never was overfond of chickens."

Poor Willie. To bring the chickens had been a real ordeal, Missie realized. She looked at him and love filled her heart. Before she could stop herself it bubbled forth.

"Willie," she said, "I love you—so much."

Willie dropped a chicken and turned to her. His eyes took on a shine.

"In thet case, Mrs. LaHaye, yer welcome to yer chickens."

Willie's surprise for his young son was a smart-looking, half-grown pup.

"He'll be a big fella when he's full-grown, an' I thought him a good idea. He'll help to keep the coyotes away from yer chickens. An' ya never know," he said with a grin, "with thet railroad a-comin; an' all those folks a-pourin in, ya never know jest who might come a-callin'. I'd feel safer iffen ya had a good watch dog."

Missie looked at the empty miles stretching before her and laughed at Willie's prediction of the crowded countryside. Suddenly she remembered that she had not told Willie of the visit from Maria.

"Willie, I *did* have a visitor—honest! A real live *woman*—though sometimes I feel thet I must have dreamed it. Oh, I wish that she'd come back. We had the best visit, an' we prayed together—"

"Where was she from?"

"I don't know."

"Ya didn't ask?"

Missie laughed.

"I asked her lots of things thet she didn't answer—or maybe *did* answer—I don't know—an' then we just gave up an' enjoyed one another."

Willie frowned.

"She couldn't understand English—an' I couldn't understand whatever it was that she spoke."

"Yet ya had ya a good visit?"

"Oh, yes."

"An' ya prayed together?"

Missie nodded in agreement.

"Yet ya couldn't understand a word thet the other spoke?"

"Not the words—but the *meanin'*. She was really nice, Willie. An' young too. An', oh, I wish so often that she'd come back— that we could have tea, an' play with Nathan, an' laugh an' pray together."

Willie put a finger under her chin and gently lifted her face until he could look into her eyes.

"I didn't realize that you were so lonesome," he said huskily. "Here I been so busy an' so taken up with the spread an' the cows an' all. I never noticed or gave thought to jest how lonesome it's been fer a woman all alone, without another female nowhere near.

"I shoulda taken ya into town, Missie. Gave ya a chance to see the outside world again, to visit an' chat. I missed yer need, Missie, an'—an' ya never complain—jest let me go on, makin' dumb mistakes right an' left. A sorry-looking bunch of cowpokes, a work-crazy husband an' a baby who can't say more than 'goo' ain't much fer company. Yet ya never, never say a thing 'bout it. I love you, too, Missie—so very much."

Chapter 33

Afternoon Tea

Missie left the house early the next morning, while Nathan slept, to fetch water for her chickens from the spring. She was determined to have eggs for the breakfast table as soon as possible. Already it promised to be a hot day and she thought of the stuffiness of the small house on such a day. Perhaps she should take Nathan to the coolness of the shade bushes near the spring for the most oppressive part of the early afternoon.

She hummed as she walked, letting the empty pail swing to and fro. She felt lighthearted this morning. Willie was home, she had heard news from dear friends; her strange new world was being enhanced, first with fresh milk, then with her bountiful garden and now with chickens. It would soon be easy to prepare good meals. She and her family would be able to enjoy many of the things that they had been accustomed to back East.

As Missie walked she reviewed parts of the letters that she had received. She again felt a pang of sadness about the misfortune of the preacher's wife. And Mrs. Taylorson! What a kind friend she had turned out to be. She had even sent a pair of tiny shoes to Nathan for when he began to walk—which wouldn't be long at the rate he was growing. Kathy's letter had been full of news of her young man. Seemed he was Samson, Solomon and the Apostle John all rolled into one. Missie smiled. But the letter that she had read and re-read was the one from Melinda. Knowing that Melinda would one day—*soon* she hoped—be near enough to be called a neighbor, was special for Missie. Oh, how she wished that Melinda were already here.

Melinda had written much about the town of Tettsford and her activities with the school and the church. She spoke of the lessening of her pain since the death of her husband, even though his memory still brought tears oftentimes. She also spoke of Henry, of his thoughtfulness, his manliness and his faith. *Yes, Missie thought, Henry truly is worthy of a girl like Melinda. They will make such delightful neighbors.*

Missie returned from the spring with the water for her chickens. She talked to them as she poured it into the trough and then portioned out the feed.

"An' you better start layin' quick-like," she threatened, "or you might find yourselves smothered in dumplin's." The chickens fought for rights at the watering trough, seeming to ignore Missie's speech.

"You are a motley-lookin' bunch," Missie said with a laugh, "but just you wait a week or two. We'll get some meat on those bones an' get those feathers smoothed out an' back where they belong. Right now you look like you're wearin' 'bout half of 'em upside down."

She picked up her pail and hurried back to the house lest Nathan awaken and miss her.

As she rounded the corner of the cookshack she found Willie and his hands gathered for a briefing. The men lounged around in various positions. Some leaned against the sod shack, others squatted on the ground, or lay propped up on an elbow. Apparently Willie had let the men know that this was a time for "at ease." Cookie sat on his bench near his cookshack door and was the first to notice Missie as she came around the corner. Missie heard Willie's voice.

"—an' as we'll all be livin' an' workin' together, I hope thet we'll feel free an' easy with one another. By now I'm sure thet you've all met Scottie, our foreman. Scottie knows all thet there is to know 'bout ranchin'. He will be takin' over the matters connected with the herd. You'll take all orders from him an' he'll be responsible to me. You are his concern an' any requests or complaints thet ya might have are directed to him. He'll see thet I hear 'bout 'em. He'll assign the shifts an' the jobs, accordin' as he sees fit. Cookie here, will feed ya. He'll have yer chow waitin' fer ya at the same time each day. There'll always be fresh coffee on, fer those comin' an' goin'—even for those on the night shift."

Willie noticed Cookie's grin and turned to see Missie standing hesitantly. His eyes lit up.

"An' now fer the bright spot on this here ranch," he said, holding out his hand to her. "I want ya to meet my wife, Mrs. LaHaye."

Missie stepped forward shyly.

"Missie," Willie said, "here're our new riders. Scottie—the foreman." Missie looked into two very kind, blue eyes, a twinkle just barely dared to show itself. Scottie looked as weathered and western as the hills that stood behind him. His small frame spoke of many years in the saddle. Missie felt a confidence in Willie's choice of man. Scottie, she felt sure, was one to be trusted.

He nodded slightly in acknowledgement of the introduction, as if to say, "Iffen ya need me, I'm here."

Missie's brief smile was a silent "Thank you."

Willie moved on. "This here is Rusty." Missie's eyes traveled to a freckled face and a mop of unruly red hair. A wide grin greeted her.

He's no more than a kid, Missie thought. Her mother heart wondered about this boy's mama and if she was somewhere worrying and praying for her son. She offered a warm smile.

"An' Smith," Willie continued. Missie turned to look into fierce black eyes in a sun-darkened face. His nod was barely perceptible and his gaze dropped quickly to the ground. *I wonder,* Missie thought, *what happened to put all that bitterness into your soul.*

"An' Brady," Willie said. Missie looked into another pair of eyes. These were cold and calculating. They raked cruelly over

Missie, making her want to blush beneath the bold stare. She nodded quickly, then gave Willie an imploring plea with her eyes to move on. She could still feel those unnerving eyes upon her.

"An' over here," Willie said, turning to the man who had risen from the ground to acknowledge the introduction, "is Lane."

Lane looked like he would gladly have allowed the earth to open up and swallow him. He started to look at Missie, changed his mind and looked at the toes of his boots instead; a dark flush spread steadily over his face. His hands sought something to do or somewhere to go but ended up only rubbing against his sides. Missie smiled. Never had she seen a man so shy. She hoped to put him at ease.

Turning from him to the others she said, "Glad to have you all here at the Hanging W," addressing herself to Scottie in particular. "I know that I won't really be seein' that much of you—you havin' your work to do, an' me havin' mine. But should there ever be a need that my husband an' I can help with, we'd be most happy to oblige." She nodded to them all, a shy smile crossing her lips. "Now I'd best get back to my baby," she said, and turned to the house.

Scottie took over the meeting and Willie walked to the soddy with Missie.

"Think I found out 'bout yer mysterious neighbor."

"Maria?"

"Yeah."

"How did you find out?"

"Scottie's already been out scoutin' the range. Says they're 'bout seven miles to the south of us. They're Mexican."

"Mexican?"

"Yep. The man speaks some English—but mostly Spanish. Prob'ly had him his own reasons fer strikin' out so far north."

"Couldn't be too serious a reason—it jest couldn't. I just know that Maria would never marry a man—"

" 'Course."

"Maybe they just wanted to be on their own—to make their own way. Lots of people feel that way, all hemmed in like by. . . ." Missie let it drop. "An' only seven miles?"

"Yep."

"That's not so far, is it, Willie? Just think! Our first neighbors—and so close. Why, I could even ride over an' see her—if I knew the way," she finished lamely.

Willie laughed. "Yeah—iffen ya knew the way. An' iffen ya didn't have to ford a river to git there. An' iffen ya knew some Spanish. *Then* ya could make a visit. But I shouldn't tease. I promise thet I'll do my best to take you over to our new neighbors. In the meantime, why don't you learn a little Spanish? It would be a real nice surprise for Maria."

"But, how can I?"

"Cookie. Cookie knows 'bout everything there is to say in the Spanish tongue. He worked fer a Spanish family when he was little more'n a kid. I got the feelin' when I heard him talk 'bout 'em he kinda wishes thet he'd stayed with 'em—but at the time he was young an' had the wander bug. He's 'bout crossed the whole continent on horseback since, it seems, workin' on spreads as he's traveled."

"Oh," said Missie, alarm showing in her voice. "I do hope that he won't decide to leave us. I—"

"Not much chance of thet. He's not as young as he used to be, nor as adventurous, either. An' I'm a thinkin' thet he don't sit a horse near as comfortable-like since he had his fall."

Missie, relieved, asked, "And he knows Spanish?"

"He sure does. Mind ya, though," Willie teased, "thet he doesn't teach ya *all* the words thet he knows. Some of 'em ain't very lady-like."

"Do you think he would—*teach* me, I mean?"

"I'm sure thet he'd be glad for an excuse to git off his bad leg occasionally."

So Missie timidly approached Cookie with regard to Spanish lessons. She had only advanced as far as *Buenos dias* and *Adios*, when Maria arrived again.

Maria cuddled Nathan, all the time directing a steady stream of flowing Spanish in turn to the baby and then to Missie. When Missie smiled and nodded, Maria's Spanish flowed even more rapidly. At length Missie could bear it no longer.

"Wait," she said to Maria. "Don't you go away—I'll be right back. You just sit right down and hug my baby. I'm gonna get us both some help."

Missie hurried out the door. She realized as she ran to the cookshack that Maria, like herself, had not understood one word of the exchange.

"Cookie," Missie said, her eyes pleading, "would you mind, please—please, would you have tea—with two ladies?"

Cookie's eyes were horror-filled.

"Oh, please," Missie begged. "Maria has come again and I can't understand her Spanish—not one word, but 'Hello.' An' she can't understand me. An' we're just dyin' to say somethin' to one another. Please, could you just—please? I'll make you coffee," Missie quickly promised.

Cookie's good-natured face crinkled into a begrudging smile. He wiped his hands on the greasy apron which he removed and cast aside.

"Iffen it means thet much."

"Oh, it does, it does."

"Fer a few minutes," Cookie agreed. "Gotta git back to the steak I'm a poundin'. But I can spare a few minutes. An' I reckon, I can pass up the coffee an' drink yer tea—long as it ain't in one of them fancy little cups."

Missie hurried with him to the sod house.

"Maria," she said triumphantly, "Here's Cookie! He knows Spanish!" When Cookie turned to Maria with a fluent welcome in her own tongue, Maria clasped her hands with a merry laugh and there was a flow of silvery-sounding Spanish.

Cookie turned to Missie and shrugged, "She says thet this is gonna be more fun than a fiesta," he said, but the look in his own eyes still indicated that he was doubtful. Missie poured his tea in a big mug and passed him some fresh bread and butter.

Cookie fell into the spirit of the game and soon seemed to be enjoying his visit almost as much as the two young women. Missie was careful to keep his mug of tea replenished and to make sure that the bread was within his reach. He didn't seem to mind even their chattering girl-talk which he had to translate coming and going.

When Maria prepared to go, the two truly did feel like *neighbors*. Missie gave her promise, through Cookie, that Willie would bring her over sometime soon.

"And Cookie?" Maria teased. Cookie muttered and grinned,

and Missie and Maria laughed.

Cookie put Nathan down, whom he had been bouncing on his knee, and declared that his time was up. But, Missie noticed, he still didn't hurry to go.

"I know you're busy, Cookie, an' I thank you so much for takin' the time. It's okay. We'll let you go now."

"Muchas gracias," Maria said, and Cookie shuffled out to return to his cookshack.

Maria's question came with actions rather than words— "Prayer?" Missie nodded.

Again the two young women of different races, different cultures, different religious backgrounds, knelt together in the small kitchen and poured their hearts out to the one true God. Missie could feel that Maria's need and longing for fellowship in the faith was as real and deep as her own.

Missie prayed, "Please, dear God, may I quickly learn enough of Maria's tongue to be able to tell her about my deep faith in You, about the life promised through the death and life of your Son. I long so much to tell her about this, to talk 'bout You, Your love and forgiveness, Your promises an' blessings. Help me, God, to learn Spanish soon." Missie added one more thought, "An' dear God, help Cookie to know the right words to teach me."

Chapter 34

Looking to Another Winter

Missie and Willie made the promised trip to their new neighbors, Maria and Juan, two weeks after Maria last visited Missie. Missie teased Cookie about accompanying them, but Scottie who could also speak a little Spanish went with them instead. When the day came for the trip, Missie felt far more inclined to ride her horse than travel in a bumpy wagon. Little Nathan was lifted up to share his father's saddle, and the four started off, Scottie setting a leisurely pace in spite of Missie's impatience to reach their destination.

The fording of the river gave Missie some butterflies, and she saw again in her mind's eye the Emorys' bobbing, tilting wagon and the plunging, terror-stricken horses. But once her horse was in and swimming strongly, Missie realized that the current was not very swift.

They found Juan and Maria living in a sprawling stone house that was cool and comfortable. Missie decided right away that she would prefer stone to any other available material. Juan was pleased to show Willie around and explain the process of building such a home. It wasn't what Missie had been used to, but it was cool against the heat of the day, and seemed so spacious after their small sod shack. Juan promised his help when the day came for Willie to build.

They left early. Mountain rains had swollen the river waters which Scottie declared to be higher than normal for the time of year, and even though it was not considered dangerous, he wanted to ford the river in full daylight.

Maria and Missie each took great comfort in knowing that there was another woman within calling distance.

When they reached home, Willie took Missie's horse and passed Nathan to her. Missie lingered outside, enjoying the coolness of the late afternoon.

Willie turned and called back to her, "Hold supper, will ya? I'm gonna ride on up to the upper spring an' see iffen it's still flowin' enough fer the cattle over thet way. I should be back in a couple of hours."

Missie agreed, glad for the extra time before lighting the fire in the stove. She placed Nathan on the ground, guiding his tottering steps toward their small home. How shabby and tiny it looked compared to Maria's. Missie would be so thankful to have more room, a floor for rugs, and windows big enough on which to hang fluttery curtains. She heard Willie's horse leave the yard as she laid Nathan down for a much-needed nap. He was sound asleep even before Missie had completed a row on the sock she was knitting.

There was a knock at her door. Missie was not used to callers. Maybe Henry had found time for a chat; she hadn't seen him since their Sunday "church" time. She stepped to the door and opened it, fully expecting Henry—or Cookie. But it was Brady. Missie fidgeted beneath the smile that he gave her and the intensity of his eyes.

"Oh," she began, but he moved past her and entered the room. Missie felt the air tighten around her.

" 'Scuse me fer intrudin', Ma'am," he said. But there was no apology in his voice. "I thought thet maybe you bein' a woman, thet ya could help me out some."

Missie remembered her lightly spoken promise of being

available to Willie's men if there was a need. A strange, fluttery feeling made her wish that she hadn't been so quick to speak. She did not move from the door.

"I seem to have picked up a sliver in my finger here, an' do ya know—there's not one of those mangy, ol' cowpokes thet has 'em a needle."

"Oh," Missie said again, and then life seemed to return to her, "Oh, yes—I have needles. Of course." Missie moved from the open door to her sewing basket, and heard the door close behind her.

She fumbled with a package of needles and finally disengaged one that she felt to be the proper size. As she rummaged her mind whirled. *What is Brady doing here? At this hour of the day all the hands are normally busy, checking cattle, mending fences, fixing gear—something. I haven't even noticed Cookie about— oh, yes, I did. As we rode up, Cookie was headin' for the spring with two water pails.*

She turned with the needle to find Brady close behind her.

"Here you are," she said, trying to keep her voice steady. But he didn't take the needle extended to him.

"I'm afraid, Ma'am, thet I'll have to ask you to be kind enough to work thet little bit of a tool fer me. My hands never were any good with anything thet size."

"Me?" Missie asked dumbly, thinking that there was no way that she was going to bend her head and work over this man's hand as she held it in her own. She could almost feel his breath upon her now in the closeness of the small room.

"I'm sorry," she said evenly. "You'll have to do it yourself— or else ask Cookie to help you."

"Now, Ma'am," the cowboy murmured, inching closer. Even in the dimness of the shanty, Missie could see his eyes seem to darken. "Don't tell me yer man-shy?"

He reached a hand out to touch her arm and Missie stepped backward, feeling the hardness of the bed as she bumped up against it. She wanted to scream, but her throat tightened in a dryness that she had never felt before. She felt her knees threatening to give way beneath her and a short prayer welled up within her. *Oh, God, strengthen me, help me, uphold me as You promised.* Then the door swung open.

"Mrs. LaHaye?" There had been no knock, but there stood Scottie. "The boss home?"

You know he's not, Missie responded to herself. *You heard him say that he was going to the upper spring.*

Instead, she said nothing. She shut her eyes to muster enough strength to remain on her feet.

"Brady?" said the foreman as though surprised. "Got those fences checked already?"

Brady turned, his eyes full of anger. Without a word he slammed out through the door. Scottie pulled out a stool for Missie. She accepted it without speaking. Then he handed her a small dipper of water; she was surprised to find that she could still swallow.

"Brady got a problem, Ma'am?" Scottie asked lightly, but Missie felt that his voice was edged with steel.

"A sliver—in his hand."

"You fix it?"

She looked down at the needle that she still held in her trembling hand and shook her head.

"I told 'im he'd have to do it himself—or get Cookie."

"Slivers bother you?"

"No," Missie replied shakily, "no, but Brady does. I don't know why. I only know—" She swallowed again. "Here," she said, holding out the needle, "would you give it to him?"

"Thet's all right, Ma'am—keep yer needle. I'll look after Brady." Then he was gone, gently closing the door behind him.

Missie sat for some time before she felt her legs strong enough to stand. At length she was able to stir herself, and build a fire to prepare Willie's supper.

She said nothing to Willie—not yet; but she vowed to keep an eye open for Brady. She'd put some kind of lock on the inside of her door if she had to. There was no way that man would enter her house again.

The next morning, as she left the house to go to the spring for water she glanced about furtively. *How dreadful not to feel safe in one's own yard,* she thought. Then she heard voices coming from the side of the bunkhouse. One was Willie's voice, and with the sound came renewed courage for Missie.

"Henry says thet Brady drew his pay."

"Yep," Scottie replied.

"Not happy ridin' fer me?"

"He didn't say nothin' 'bout bein' unhappy."

"But he quit?"

"Nope." And after a pause, "I fired 'im."

"Thought he was known to be *good* with cattle." Willie's voice seemed to suggest a shrug of his shoulders as though he couldn't quite understand the situation, but Scottie was boss where the cowhands were concerned.

"Reckon he was." Scottie was noncommittal.

"Reckon you had yer reasons," Willie said.

"Yeah," Scottie said softly, "reckon I did."

Missie continued on her way to the spring. Her world suddenly belonged to her again—her garden, her chickens, her house. She could count on Willie's men to care not only for his cattle but to care for her as well. And with Willie's men and her Heavenly Father, she really had no need to worry. None at all.

Missie placed a chair in the shade of the sod house and continued her work on a pair of trousers for Nathan. His dog lay nearby, already grown almost to full size. The black mongrel showed some intelligence, and was ever so gentle with young Nathan. For the gentleness, Missie allowed him her devotion.

It was cool in the evenings now, and Missie was thankful for the relief from the intense summer heat. For many days she had been busy canning the produce from her garden; and as she watched it stack up around her, she began to wonder where she would keep it from freezing over the long winter. Unless she could persuade Willie to dig a root cellar, they would have to bury the food in the hay in the barn. Missie wished again for a new, bigger house, but she held her tongue. She knew that it would be hers as soon as Willie was able.

She looked up from her work and saw Henry approaching.

"Hi, stranger," she teased. "I had begun to wonder if you were still ridin' for this outfit. I haven't seen you for so long."

"It's this boss I got," Henry responded. "Don't know nothin' but work, work, work!"

Missie laughed.

"But then," Henry added, "guess he can't be all bad. He's promised me two weeks off."

"Really? Ya makin' a trip?"

Henry flushed with pleasure. "I sure am," he offered. "Jest as fast as ol' Flint can carry me. Seems like downright years. . . .'"

"I'm so happy for you an' Melinda," Missie said. "She must be missin' you somethin' awful, too."

"I sure hope so," Henry said. "Iffen she misses me half as much. . . ." Again he let the sentence hang.

"Have you set a date?" Missie asked, "Or am I bein' nosy?"

"Don't mind yer interest none. An' no, not yet. Sure wish thet we could, but it depends."

"On what?"

"On how soon I can build a house."

"With a little help, you can have a house up in a few days."

"I mean a *house*, Missie, not a sod shanty."

Missie was surprised at the intensity of Henry's reply.

"I agree," she said carefully, "that there's not much invitin' 'bout a sod shanty, but it can be a home—be it ever so simple an' confinin'."

"I'd never ask Melinda to live in such conditions—never." Henry said vehemently. "Don't you think thet I saw the look in yer eyes when ya spotted the dirt floor, the dingy windows, the crowded—" but Missie stopped him.

"Henry," she said softly, "answer me true. Do you still see that look there now? That look of surprise, of hurt, of disappointment? Is it still there?"

Henry paused, then shook his head. "No," he said, "I guess not. You've done well, Missie. Really great—an' I've admired ya fer it. A girl like you—leavin' what ya had, an' comin' way out here to this. I've truly admired ya. But, beggin' yer pardon—I won't ask thet of Melinda."

"An' I respect you for your thoughtfulness concernin' her, Henry. But you should know something." Missie stopped to choose her words carefully. "Henry, I want you to know that I'd far sooner share this little one-room dirt dwellin' with Willie than to live in the world's fanciest big white house without him. An' I mean that, Henry."

Henry chuckled softly to hide the depth of his feelings.

"You women are strange creatures, indeed," he said. "No wonder we men never succeed in understandin' ya. But thanks be to God fer makin' ya the way ya are. Ya really do mean thet, don't ya?"

"I really do," Missie said. And deep in her heart she marvelled at just how much she meant it. The glory of the truth somehow unshackled her spirit from the small, shabby little dwelling, to soar far above it in the strength of her love for Willie. Somehow, the long, dreaded winter ahead did not look so frightening now, even though she still faced being shut away in the one, confining room. She and Willie and Nathan might be crowded together, but they were bundled comfortably in the blanket of love.

Chapter 35

Sundays

When Henry returned from visiting his Melinda, Missie sensed about him a loneliness that he never had to express. She wondered if he was silently realizing that perhaps love could have seen them through a winter in a little sod house; but Henry never admitted as much. He missed Melinda—that was very evident. He often found excuses to drop by the sod shanty and chat or play with Nathan to help fill the lonely hours.

Henry and the young Rusty seemed to enjoy one another's company as well, and often rode out together. Missie knew that Scottie wisely tried to team up the men who worked well together. In the evenings in the bunkhouse, Henry was teaching Rusty to strum his guitar. The two young cowboys spent many hours singing range songs and old hymns.

One Sunday as Willie, Missie and Henry sat talking after their usual time of Bible study and prayer, they discussed the coming railroad, the people it would bring, future shops, schools and even a doctor.

Then Willie said with deep feeling, "Ya know what I long fer most? A church. I jest ache sometimes to gather with a group of believers and sing an' pray an' read the Word. It seems like so long—what I wouldn't give fer jest one Sunday back home."

Missie's eyes became misty. A Sunday back home meant Pa with his baritone voice expressing his praise, Ma in her quiet, confident manner joining in. It meant Clare and Arnie, Ellie and little Luke gathered 'round. It meant Nandry and Clae and their families. Missie wondered if there were more members to the families now, how tall Clare was, if Arnie still teased Ellie, and if everyone still spoiled little Luke. She wondered if Marty still looked west each night and breathed a prayer for her faraway little girl, and if Pa still lifted down the family Bible and read with a steady, assured voice the promises of God. Were they all well— her family? If only there was some way to span the miles, as Willie had put it, to spend a Sunday at home.

Missie blinked away her tears, and came back to the reality of her small home.

"It would be so good to hear the Word with others," Willie was saying. "I'll be so glad when we have enough neighbors to have our own little church and a preacher."

Then Willie was looking around the room, seeming to size it up.

"Remember how we all managed to crowd in here fer Christmas?"

"Yeah, we were toe to toe—but we fit," Missie laughed.

"Well, we can fit again," Willie said. "Boy, have I been dumb!"

He reached for his hat. "Put on the coffeepot, Missie," he said. "I'm gonna go fer the *congregation*, and he ducked quickly through the door.

And so it was that all the hands that worked on the Hanging W Ranch were invited to share in Sunday services in the little sod house.

That first Sunday only Rusty came with Henry, but what a time they had singing the old hymns accompanied by Henry's guitar, and reading the Scriptures together. The next Sunday, it was Henry and Rusty again.

A couple of Sundays later, Cookie hobbled in, clearing his

throat and looking embarrassed at his weakness in getting so near to "religion."

In spite of the ridicule that came from the hardened Smith (who, whenever he was asked his full name snapped, "It's Smith—jest Smith," making Missie wonder if he really had a claim to even that), the weeks passed with the little meeting growing. On Christmas Sunday, Smith was the only holdout. He saddled his horse and rode away into the quietness of the snow-covered hills. Missie prayed that God might somehow reach his cold, unhappy heart.

After their service together, Missie managed to serve them a special Christmas dinner. She had even been tempted to sacrifice two of her chickens for the occasion, but could not bring herself to do so. She was getting four or five eggs a day, and as she still hadn't determined who were the producers and who were the sluggards, she granted them all extended life, lest she take the wrong ones.

With her milk, eggs and some hoarded raisins, she made some bread pudding. Even those who did not care for the chickens themselves did not scorn what the hens were able to produce. And they smacked their lips as they went back for seconds.

Nathan, having passed the milestone of his first birthday, thoroughly enjoyed the whole crowded celebration. He shook his head sadly when the last figure left the small shack. "A' gone," he sighed, "A' gone."

After having made the plunge for Christmas Sunday, the last loners seemed reluctant to avoid the regular Sunday services. Unless duty called them away, at the appointed time of two o'clock they all, but Smith, entered the house, dusting the snow from their coats with their hats as they walked in stamping their boots. Then they filed quietly to their places for the short time of singing, Bible reading and prayer.

Missie prayed that Rusty, the easy-going, open-hearted young boy of the group, would desire more than just a Sunday gathering. He eagerly sang the old hymns and listened attentively as the Scripture was read.

To Missie's surprise, it was the shy, backward Lane who knocked on their door one evening and asked in an embarrassed and stumbling voice, "Is the boss in?"

Missie ushered him in and he stood facing Willie, nervously twisting his hat in his hand.

"I wondered, Boss, iffen y'all would mind—iffen you'd—" he cleared his throat. "I don't have much understandin' 'bout the things of the Bible. Could ya—would ya sorta go over it again—slow-like, iffen ya don't mind?"

So Lane was invited to sit down at the table, and by the dim light of the flickering lamp, with fresh cups of coffee before them, he and Willie again went over the words of the Book.

"If thou shalt confess with thy mouth the Lord Jesus, and shalt believe in thine heart that God hath raised him from the dead, thou shalt be saved."*

Missie sat off to the side, her hands finding jobs to do for which she needed little light. She prayed that God would bless His Word, and open the understanding of the young man.

Her heart was full. God had been good to Willie and her. And He had given them their own unique, yet special, *congregation*.

---

*Romans 10:9, KJV.

Chapter 36

Dreams

Missie's second winter in the soddy was nearing its end.

The winter winds seemed to be abating, and she even dared to hope for an early thaw. Already she was mentally planning her garden, though she knew full well that it would be weeks before she could actually do the planting. This year, she promised herself, she would listen to Willie and not rush it so. But secretly, she wondered if her wisdom could hold her eagerness in check.

This spring she hoped to have some setting hens as well; and though she had still made use of her daily egg supply, she had been holding some back each day for the settings. A spring calf was due to Ginger, their milk cow; in no way could the dozens of range calves expected compare to the anticipation of that one calf that would be born to the cow in the barn. Pansy still was milked daily, although her supply was running low. It would soon be her turn to take a rest from the daily production and wait for her calf which was still some months away.

And then there was the promised house to look forward to! Missie had fretted about it so, fearing that the money shouldn't be spent on one for another year—but Willie was determined that the start be made on the stone home as soon as possible. A good share of the outer material was almost free, he assured her, and the labor would be cheap.

With Scottie to oversee the activities of the ranch, Willie would be free to get on with the building. Juan also had promised him two helpers who had a great deal of experience with stone buildings. Willie sat at night at the small table and drew up plans for the house. The low, rambling stone building would be built with the main living area in the middle, the kitchen and dining area located in the left wing and the bedrooms in the right. A shaded porch and small courtyard would provide a good spot for Missie to sit and do handwork while young Nathan enjoyed the out-of-doors. Willie discussed the plans with Missie and then redrew them, over and over. Missie tried to restrain herself, not daring to let it become too real, lest something happen that would prevent the carrying out of their plans.

But she did her share of dreaming.

Oh, the fun she would have unpacking all their stored things—the proper-sized stove, the sewing machine, the rugs, the curtains, the fancy dishes. At times she thought that she would burst in her eagerness.

Henry had decided that with the spring, he also would do some building. He had obtained the land bordering Willie's and had plans to put his house just as close to the LaHayes' home as he could, so that it would be convenient for the women to visit and do things together. Missie could scarcely wait for Melinda to arrive.

Willie agreed to sell Henry fifty head of cattle, with whatever calves were at heel, so that Henry could get a start on his spread.

This would also give Willie some cash for the new house. If Scottie disapproved of a cattleman making sales in the spring, he did not say so. He knew that the sale would assist both men in realizing their dreams.

Rusty decided to go to work on Henry's spread, so Scottie needed to find two more hands for the Hanging W. He assured Willie that he would take his time and choose carefully.

Scottie reported that the outlying ranches were already planning a fall trail drive to move their cattle to the market. If Willie wanted to, he could send as many head of cattle as he wished, along with a designated number of riders. Willie decided that he'd hold his herd that year unless unexpected expenses demanded more cash. Everyone was hopeful that before another fall rolled around, the railroad would have made its promised appearance. This would eliminate the costly, time-consuming, wearying trail drive.

The winter losses seemed to be low and the calf crop looked good. As each count came in, Missie's hopes for the new home mounted.

Missie anticipated the summer before her, with even the thought of the approaching heat not able to wither her spirits.

She gazed across the endless hills. She and Willie had lived in the area such a short time and already they were seeing changes—and the future promised many more. Would they all come true—the dreams, the plans? Whatever the outcome, things were going well now. She was sure, for the first time, that if they really needed to, they could carry on indefinitely just as they had been living.

She decided that as soon as Nathan woke from his nap she'd ride up for a look at the mountains. She was wondering what color they would appear on this bright, spring-like morning.

Cookie appeared at the cookshack door carrying a dishpan. He tossed the water carelessly to the side of the path and stopped to look at the sky. Missie wondered if he also was coaxing spring to come.

Chapter 37

Nathan

Willie went to check the horses before retiring, while Missie finished the dishes and prepared Nathan for bed.

"You are gettin' so big," she said. "Soon you aren't gonna fit in that wee bed anymore. Your pa is gonna have to make you a bigger one."

Nathan smiled, "Big boy."

Missie kissed his chubby cheeks.

"Big boy, all right. Mama's big boy."

Nathan returned her kiss in his wet, yet affectionate fashion.

"Now," Missie said, "let's say our prayers."

Missie prayed, stopping often to let Nathan try to repeat her words. He finished with a hearty " 'men." As Missie bundled him into bed, she noticed that his breathing sounded heavier than usual.

"I do hope that you're not comin' down with a cold," she told him. "Won't be long now until the days will be nice an' sunny an' warm, and you can go outside to play as much as you like."

"Doggie?"

"Sure, you can play with your doggie. You always think of 'doggie' when I talk about outside, don't you? Well, soon now you can be out with Max as much as you want to."

Nathan seemed to like the idea.

Missie tucked him in and kissed him again, then began to re-fill the lamp with oil. Willie might wish to work on his house plans again.

Willie returned and, as Missie expected, pulled his stool up to the table. He still wasn't sure that the entrance to the house was in the most convenient place. He tried various drawings, first shifting it one way and then the other. Missie watched and made suggestions while she darned a sock. Willie finally decided that his first choice had been the right one.

They went to bed early. The next day's branding was bound to be long and tiring.

Missie lay for a few moments listening to Nathan's breathing, then Willie's snoring drowned out the sound. She felt a tightening in her stomach as she turned over to try to go to sleep, but couldn't decide just why.

Missie wasn't sure who awakened first—she or Willie; but she suddenly realized that she was sitting upright in bed, a feeling of horror making her blood pound in her ears. Already Willie was springing from the bed.

"What is it?" Missie called in the dark.

"It's Nathan! He's chokin' somethin' awful."

Missie heard it then—the rattling gasp for breath.

"Oh, God, no!" she cried, and tumbled out of bed after Willie.

"Light the lamp," Willie ordered, already reaching for the small boy.

Missie hurried to fetch it, her bare feet feeling the coolness of the dirt floor.

"What is it? What's the matter with him, Willie?"

"Was he okay when ya put him to bed?"

"He was a little heavy-soundin', but nothin' like—Oh, dear God, what can we do? What is it, Willie?" Missie cried, her heart tearing at each ragged breath of her small baby.

No doctor! her heart screamed with each wild beat. No doctor! Not for miles and miles! No help anywhere near here!

"Have you ever seen this before in any of yer family?" Willie asked frantically.

"Never!" replied Missie, the tears running down her cheeks. "Never! I've no idea what it be. Unless—could it be pneumonia? He can't breathe." *Oh, dear God, we need You now,* her heart cried. *Little Nathan Isaiah needs You now. Please, dear God, show us what to do, or send us some help—someone who knows. Please, God.*

"Have ya some medicine?" implored Willie. "Some things from yer ma? Where do ya keep it, Missie?"

"All I ever brought in were the first-aid supplies. There's more still stored in the barn, though. I've never unpacked it—never needed it—'till now."

"I'll git it—ya stay and keep 'im warm, Missie."

"No, Willie, you wouldn't know the box—it'll take you too long to find it. I'll go, I know just where it is."

Missie pulled on her boots and shoved her arms into the sleeves of Willie's coat, then quickly lit another lantern. She ran from the house, the mud and slush from the spring puddles splashing on her bare legs.

"Oh, dear God," her prayer continued, "please help us. We don't have a doctor. We don't even have a neighbor near. We don't know what to do. Please help us, God. I couldn't bear to lose him. I just couldn't, God." The tears poured down her cheeks.

She found the box of medicines quickly enough and ran with it back to the house, still pleading, "Oh, please, God, please save my baby."

As she neared the shanty she could see inside through the tiny window. Willie stood with the baby in his arms. He was praying. Missie saw his tears and the anguish on his face.

"Oh, dear God," she prayed, coming to a sudden stop. "It's Willie's *son,* his pride and joy, God. If You must take our baby—be with my Willie. Give 'im the strength to bear it, God. He loves his boy so much. Oh, dear God, please help us, please, please help us—if only someone knew—" and she hurried into the house.

She placed the box on the table. Without removing her heavy

coat she frantically clawed at the lid with a hammer from a peg near the door. The lid came loose with a loud squeak.

She rummaged through the medicines, having no idea what she should be looking for. Willie paced the floor holding the young Nathan upright in an effort to ease his troubled breathing. Suddenly there was a "hullo" outside the door and, without even waiting for a reply, Cookie burst in.

He did not ask questions. His eyes and ears had already taken in the answers.

"Croup!" he said explosively.

"What?" Willie exclaimed.

"Croup."

"You know what it is?"

"Sure do. Thet breathin'—thet's croup."

"Can you—?" Missie was afraid to ask.

"Can sure try. Git the fire goin'. Make it as hot as ya can and git some water boilin' fast."

Willie handed the struggling baby to Missie and hurried to comply. He filled the stove with cow chips and soaked them with fuel from the lamp. A brisk fire was soon blazing. Willie set the kettle directly over the flame, though it still seemed to take forever to boil.

Cookie placed a stool in the middle of the room.

"Git me a blanket."

Willie whipped a blanket from their bed.

"Now we need a basin fer the water."

Willie pulled the dishpan from its hook.

Cookie busily dug through the medicines that Missie had strewn across the table. He carefully read labels that had been placed on each one by Missie's mother.

"This oughta do," Cookie said. "Got a spoon?"

Willie handed him a spoon and Cookie poured out a large helping of the ointment and dumped it into the basin. The water finally boiling, Cookie poured it into the pan and held out his arms for the baby. Missie was reluctant, but Cookie seemed to be their only hope. She passed over her small son.

"Put some more water on and keep thet fire goin'," Cookie ordered and sat himself down on the stool.

"Now push thet basin over here, an' toss thet blanket over the both of us. We gotta have us a good steam bath."

They covered the two of them and then waited silently. Willie poked at the fire and Missie paced the floor in the small space left to her, listening painfully to Nathan's choking, rasping efforts to breathe. The minutes ticked by. From beneath the heavy blanket came Cookie's voice, startling both Willie and Missie.

"Thet other water boilin' yet?"

It was.

"Pull out this here basin an' change the water. Put in another scoop of the medicine, too."

It was done, and Willie pushed the steaming pan back under the blanket tent, being careful not to release the build-up of steam already trapped within.

Again Missie paced and prayed, while Willie poked at the fire and prayed. He stuffed in another chip every time that he could make one fit. The room was becoming unbearably hot.

Nathan began to fuss. *Was he worse?* Panic seized Missie.

"Good sign," Cookie called out. "Before, he was too busy fightin' fer breath to bother to fight the steam. His breathin' seems to be easin' some."

It has, Missie thought with wild joy. *He's not chokin' near as much.* Her tears began to fall as she repeated softly to herself, "Fear thou not; for I am with thee: be not dismayed; for I am thy God. I will strengthen thee; yea, I will help thee—" Missie could go no further. Sobs of thankfulness were crowding out all other thought. "Oh, dear God, thank You, thank You."

Willie made another change of water, passing it to Cookie beneath the blanket. Nathan stopped fussing and his breathing steadily improved.

"He's asleep now," Cookie announced in a loud whisper. "He seems able to breathe without too much strugglin'."

Missie's arms ached to hold her baby but Cookie kept him under the blanket.

The first streaks of dawn were reaching their golden fingers toward the eastern hills before Cookie ventured to lift the blanket from his head.

"Put on the coffeepot, would ya, Missus?" was his only comment.

Willie reached to take away the blanket and move the basin.

Missie moved mechanically to fill the coffeepot and put it on the stove. She then turned to Cookie who was handing the sleeping baby to this father.

"Put him back to bed now," he said, then added slowly, "This might come again fer a night or two, but iffen yer watchin' fer it, ya should be able to ward it off. In a few nights' time he should be over it. Croup always hits like thet—in the dead of night, scarin' one half to death. The steamin' helps."

Missie looked at the little man. He spoke quietly, matter-of-factly, as though he were used to working miracles. His body appeared limp; his clothes were soaked with steam and perspiration, his wispy hair clung wet against his scalp. His face was drained and white, and glistened with moisture in the early morning light. Yet, Missie's heart cried out that he was truly the most beautiful person that she had ever seen.

She crossed the room and reached out to touch gently his soft, stubbled face.

"Cookie Adams," she said, with tears and laughter in her voice, "you can't fool me—not for a minute. You're no grouchy, hard-ridin' ole cowpoke a'tall. You're a visitin' *angel*."

Chapter 38

Love Finds a Home

Missie finally planted her garden and set her hens. Green things soon appeared and so did soft, fluffy, yellow chicks—eighteen of them; and Missie rejoiced, thinking ahead to leafy vegetables and fried chicken. Even Willie admitted that her idea of raising chickens was not such a bad one after all. The cow calved, a fine young heifer. Missie's milk supply was assured for many months ahead.

Willie, under the instruction of Juan and his men, began the work on the house, just a few yards east of the sod shanty. Day after day Missie watched excitedly as it took shape.

Henry had left for his own ranch. Missie missed him and the redheaded Rusty. She was always glad to welcome them back for a visit or a meal. Henry and Rusty still joined them each Sunday, and Missie and Willie were glad to have them. She wasn't sure yet how Willie's two new hands felt about working on a spread where the boss had Sunday sing-songs and Bible reading. So far, they had chosen to follow Smith's leading and stay away from such going's on.

Willie took time from his house-building to ride over to Juan's for a meeting of cattlemen. Missie ached to go along, but knew that the visiting of women and a business meeting of the men might not mix too well. She contented herself with plans for a visit on some future day, when she and Maria could enjoy each other's company without interruption. Maria's English was improving even faster than Missie's Spanish, and the two young women spent much of their infrequent visits laughing at each other's mistakes.

When Willie returned he was fairly bursting with news. A group of men had been in to stake out a site for the train station, he told Missie. Land already was sold for a general store. He was certain that other buildings would follow. And the best news was that the station would be only fifteen miles away! An easy trip in one day! No more two-week supply trips to Tettsford Junction. The first train was due to come chugging in during early spring of the following year.

The thought took Missie's breath away. To have supplies come in so close, to be able to make a trip to town, to greet people and walk on sidewalks—it was all too overwhelming to comprehend.

"Sure, it'll take time—but it'll all come," Willie declared. "An' guess what else. Thet there train station is gonna be more'n jest a cattle-shippin' place. It's gonna have a post office, too. We'll be able to mail letters right here an' git answers back from our folks."

Missie caught her breath. Just to be able to write home to her mama and pa! To be able to tell them of Nathan's progress, of her new house, of Cookie—their faithful old ranch hand sent to them by God himself (though Cookie didn't realize that yet), of her chickens, her garden. Oh, how she wanted to tell them everything, to pour it all out on paper, letting them know and feel that she was doing just fine. And to get back an answer from them assuring her that they were all well. She tried to imagine their first letter: that Luke was almost a man now, that Ellie had herself a beau, that Clare was getting set up to go farming on his own, and that Arnie was busy working the plow for Pa. She wanted to hear that the apple trees were in blossom, and the ever-bubbling spring had just been cleaned for the summer cooling, that soft green lay on the land, and the school bell was ringing clearly in the crisp morning air.

Missie's eyes softened with her musings.

"Oh, Willie," she said, "I'd never even thought of such a wonder."

"An' I been thinkin'," Willie hardly dared to say more, in case it were a dream that would never be realized. "Been thinkin'—not a reason in the world thet I can see, why yer folks couldn't jest hop thet train some day an' make a trip out here."

"Oh, Willie," Missie cried, "could they really? Could people—it's not just for cows?"

Willie laughed. " 'Course not. At the meetin' they said thet they 'spect lots of folks will be comin' out by train. Special car jest for folks to ride in—maybe even two cars iffen they be needin' 'em. Yer folks could come right on out an' we could meet 'em at the station."

Missie caught hold of his sleeve. "It's too much—too much all at once. I feel I could burst if it doesn't stop."

"Don't ya go bustin'," Willie said, pulling her to him. "We still got no doctor—an' I need ya. Who else is gonna look after Nathan an' me, an' git thet there house a lookin' like a home, 'stead of an empty, bare shell?" He chuckled as he held her close.

Missie was content to rest quietly in his arms.

"Speakin' of houses," Willie said against her hair, "iffen it's gonna be ready fer yer folks, I'd best git back to buildin' it. I decided today to send twenty or thirty steers along on thet cattle drive. No use doin' a thing by half-measures. Soon as Scottie gits back with the money, I'll take one of the boys an' head fer Tettsford. An' this time, I'm takin' you too, Missie. Iffen I don't git you away from this all-male company, you'll be losing all yer feminine charms!" But his eyes told her he didn't think that was likely.

Missie laughed, then retorted primly, "Why, yes, I believe I will be able to join you on your trip to Tettsford." But her dancing eyes gave her away, and she laughed again for sheer joy.

"We can git our winter supplies at the same time," Willie added.

"I need more preservin' jars," Missie said. "Mercy! I planted more garden then either Cookie or I know what to do with."

Willie chuckled and released her.

"You be thinkin' on yer list," he said. "We'll be doin' our best to be fillin' it." He picked up his tools and started off for the new house. As he went he whistled, and the sound of it was pleasant to Missie's ears.

Around the corner of the cookshack limped Cookie, and close behind him trailed the young Nathan, followed by his ever-present guardian, big Max.

Nathan chattered and Cookie grunted. The dog was content to be the silent partner, giving an occasional wag of his tail.

Missie turned back to the little sod house. It was time to build a fire and begin preparing the evening meal. As she walked, she mentally composed her first letter home.

"Dear Mama and Pa," she'd write.

"God truly has kept His promise of Isaiah 41:10, just as you said He would. You should see our Nathan. He's about the greatest boy that ever was. He's quick too, in learning and doing. You'd be real proud of your grandson. I think that his nose and chin are like Willie's, but he has *your* eyes, Pa.

"Truth is, we're expecting another baby. Not for several months yet, but we're excited about it. We haven't talked yet about what we'll do for the birthing and all, but maybe by then we'll have folks around and I won't have to go way back to Tettsford Junction. I pray that that might be so.

"Willie is building a stone house—our *real* house. The one that we've been living in, temporarily, is kind of small. It's been just fine though, but now we're getting all set to move into the new one. We want to be in before winter comes again.

"I have a nice big garden. It grows real well down by the spring. The soil is rich and easy to water there. I scarcely have to coax it along at all. Cookie, the cook, uses it for the ranch hands as well.

"I have chickens, too. This spring they gave us eighteen chicks and we only lost two; I get seven or eight eggs a day. We're going to have chicken for Christmas dinner this year!

"And we have neighbors! Maria is the closest one to the

south. She is a very good friend and we have enjoyed prayer times together. Soon Melinda, a friend from the wagon train, will live to the north of us. You remember our Henry, the driver that you found for us, Pa? Well, he met Melinda on the trip out here, and as soon as he finishes his house, they will be married. I can hardly wait.

"We have a real good ranch foreman, Scottie, and a number of men who work the spread. There is Cookie—I mentioned him before—who is Nathan's favorite—mine too; and Lane, Smith, Clem, Sandy and two new ones whom I still don't know very well. The new ones haven't yet been to our Sunday Bible reading but we're still praying. Their names are Jake and Walt. Of course they all have last names too, except Smith, but we hardly ever use them here. Pray for all of them. Lane has become a real believer but takes a lot of ribbing from Smith. It would really help him if Jake and Walt broke from Smith and started coming on Sunday too. Especially pray for Smith. He really needs God to thaw out his heart."

Missie pushed the kettle onto the heat and went outside for a new supply of chips. Her eyes traveled over the miles of hills. They were not just distant, barren knolls now, but separate, individual. She remembered the coyote that appeared on that closest one. She had gazed at the one to the northeast when she looked for Willie's returning team. On the far ones she often saw the cattle feeding. The ones close by were covered with beautiful spring flowers. She'd transplanted some of them around the sod shanty door and watered them faithfully with her dishwater, almost always remembering Mrs. Taylorson's Rule Number Four, "All water must be used *at least twice. . . .*"

She turned her eyes toward the west. Even though she could not see them from her valley, her memory brought to mind the mountains—shadowy, misty and golden, by turn. "Like a woman," Willie teased, "always changin' in mood and appearance."

She turned back to the hills. How pretty they looked. In the distance were dots, that she knew to be Willie's grazing cattle. A faster-moving black figure appeared for a moment and then disappeared over a rise—one of the hands checking on the herd. Another cowboy rode into the yard down by the corrals. Missie heard the thud of the hoofbeats and saw little smoky swirls of dust. She had missed her ride that morning. She would be sure to take Nathan on out on the morrow. The sting of the wind on her face and the smell of sage in the air always awakened her and sent her home, eager to begin her day of scrubbing clothes or canning vegetables.

"You know," her letter would go on, "how Willie boasted of his land when he came back? Well, it's even prettier than that. I didn't see it that way at first, but I love it now. The air is so crisp and clean, you can almost serve it on a platter. And the distant mountains change their dress as regularly as a high-fashion city lady."

Missie filled her pail, hoisted it up and started for the sod dwelling.

"Willie brought wonderful news today," her mental letter continued. "He says that the railroad which is coming soon will not only haul out cattle but will bring people as well. He says that you'll be able to come right on out here for a visit. Can you imagine that? I could hardly believe it at first, and now I can hardly wait. I never dreamed when I left back east that I'd ever be able to show you my home."

Missie's eyes filled with unbidden tears. "My home," she said softly, realizing that she had never said the words about this place before. "My home! It truly is! I don't feel the awful tug back east anymore—this is truly *my home*—mine an Willie's." Joy and pride filled her heart.

I can hardly wait to show 'em, her thoughts tumbled over each other. *They'll love it. It's so beautiful—the mountains, the hills, the spring—I wonder if an apple tree would grow down by the spring? I could have Pa bring out some cuttings—it wouldn't hurt none to try.*

Missie turned back to the temporary sod shanty that had been her home for two whole years.

"You know," she said to the building, "I'll almost miss you. I think I'll ask Willie to leave you sittin' here. You can be my quiet place an' I can come here sometimes an' think an' remember— the Christmas dinners when we crammed in here all together; Cookie a-sittin' there on that stool nursin' Nathan back to us; the plannin' that Willie did at that little table; the dreams, the tears, the fears that we've shared here. I've done a heap of growin' since I entered this door—an' there's still more to do—I reckon."

Missie looked about her. What else would she tell her Mama and Pa? Maybe very little more. Maybe it was best for them to come and see for themselves. It was hard to put hopes and dreams on sheets of paper. Dreams of a future holding a church and a school for Nathan and his brothers and sisters. Dreams of white curtains and a sunlit sewing room. Dreams of Willie with a herd the size he had always planned for. Dreams of neighbors and friends, laughter and shared recipes.

It would be hard to put her dreams down in neat rows of writing. It would be so much better when she could open her door and her arms to her mama and pa and say, "Welcome! Welcome to my home. There's love here. Love that started growing 'way back on the farm, an' traveled all the way here with us, growin' an' strengthenin' every mile of the way. *God's* love—just as He promised. *Your* love, for us as your children. And *our* love for one another and for our son. Love! That's what makes a home. So, welcome, Mama and Pa. Welcome to our love-filled home."